HARBOR FESTIVAL

STARLIGHT SHORES
BOOK TWO

KAY CORRELL

ZURA LU PUBLISHING LLC

High-powered marketing executive Cassidy Wren didn't plan to spend her mandatory, so-called *vacation* in a sleepy coastal town—especially not one with a failing festival and opinions about everything.

Burned out, bitter, and convinced her career is slipping away, Cassidy arrives in Starlight Shores determined to endure her time at the quaint seaside cottage, build a comeback plan, and return to corporate life. But when the mayor learns of her marketing background, Cassidy is strong-armed into reviving the town's struggling annual Harbor Festival, a beloved event tied to the community's maritime heritage.

From the start, Cassidy clashes with Bryan Lucas, a third-generation fisherman and head of the festival committee. Bryan is fiercely protective of the working waterfront and deeply suspicious of Cassidy's big-city ideas. As planning unfolds, their professional tension gives way to reluctant respect and a growing attraction neither expected.

While researching the festival's past, Cassidy uncovers old photographs showing the lighthouse hosting mysterious academic visitors in the past. Winnie, the lighthouse keeper, offers only half-answers, hinting at a past no one seems eager to discuss.

As storms threaten festival preparations and outside developers circle the lighthouse, the town bands together. Working alongside neighbors who quickly become friends, Cassidy discovers something she never found in corporate success: a true sense of belonging.

When her boss arrives with a promotion that would pull her away just as the festival begins, Cassidy must choose between the life she planned and the community she's grown to love.

Set against the warm, windswept coast of Florida, *Harbor Festival,* book two in the Starlight Shores series, is a heartwarming small-town romance about community, second chances, found family, and the secrets a lighthouse keeps. Perfect for readers who love cozy coastal fiction, gentle romance, and stories where belonging matters more than ambition.

between series - with Josephine and Paul from The Letter.)

LIGHTHOUSE POINT ~ THE SERIES
Wish Upon a Shell - Book One
Wedding on the Beach - Book Two
Love at the Lighthouse - Book Three
Cottage near the Point - Book Four
Return to the Island - Book Five
Bungalow by the Bay - Book Six
Christmas Comes to Lighthouse Point - Book Seven

CHARMING INN ~ Return to Lighthouse Point
One Simple Wish - Book One
Two of a Kind - Book Two
Three Little Things - Book Three
Four Short Weeks - Book Four
Five Years or So - Book Five
Six Hours Away - Book Six
Charming Christmas - Book Seven

SWEET RIVER ~ THE SERIES
A Dream to Believe in - Book One
A Memory to Cherish - Book Two
A Song to Remember - Book Three
A Time to Forgive - Book Four
A Summer of Secrets - Book Five
A Moment in the Moonlight - Book Six

MOONBEAM BAY ~ THE SERIES

The Parker Women - Book One

The Parker Cafe - Book Two

A Heather Parker Original - Book Three

The Parker Family Secret - Book Four

Grace Parker's Peach Pie - Book Five

The Perks of Being a Parker - Book Six

BLUE HERON COTTAGES ~ THE SERIES

Memories of the Beach - Book One

Walks along the Shore - Book Two

Bookshop near the Coast - Book Three

Restaurant on the Wharf - Book Four

Lilacs by the Sea - Book Five

Flower Shop on Magnolia - Book Six

Christmas by the Bay - Book Seven

Sea Glass from the Past - Book Eight

MAGNOLIA KEY ~ THE SERIES

Saltwater Sunrise - Book One

Encore Echoes - Book Two

Coastal Candlelight - Book Three

Tidal Treasures - Book Four

Bayside Beginnings - Book Five

Seaside Sunshine - Book Six

Boardwalk Breezes - Book Seven

STARLIGHT SHORE ~ THE SERIES

Lighthouse Cottages - Book One

Harbor Festival - Book Two

Coastal Shadows - Book Three

CHRISTMAS SEASHELLS AND SNOWFLAKES

Seaside Christmas Wishes

Sweet River Holiday Homecoming

WIND CHIME BEACH ~ A stand-alone novel

INDIGO BAY ~

Sweet Days by the Bay - Kay's Complete Collection of stories in the Indigo Bay series

Sign up for my newsletter at my website *kaycorrell.com* to make sure you don't miss any new releases or sales.

CHAPTER 1

The sunrise over the Gulf was stunning. Cassidy Wren knew this because the wellness blog she'd bookmarked had specifically recommended watching sunrises as a therapeutic practice for high-functioning professionals in recovery from burnout.

She sat on the upper balcony of Heron Cottage with her tablet propped on her knees. The spreadsheet glowed against the soft dawn light. She'd color-coded her sabbatical schedule by activity type. Blue for physical wellness. Green for mental health. Yellow for creative exploration.

Six o'clock. Sunrise Reflection. Check.

Her smartwatch buzzed. Heart rate: 79 bpm. Still elevated for someone supposedly relaxing.

She tried the breathing exercise from the app. Four counts in. Hold for seven. Eight counts out.

Her chest tightened instead of releasing. She was doing relaxation wrong. There had to be a more efficient method.

The waves rolled against the shore beyond the lighthouse. Rhythmic. Predictable. The kind of sound people paid good money to download for sleep aids.

She just wanted to throw her tablet at them.

The silence was unbearable. In Chicago, her mornings started with the rumble from the L, the coffee cart vendor's greeting, and the elevator's digital chime. Her calendar pinged every fifteen minutes. Her phone buzzed with Slack notifications before she'd finished her first latte. The noise meant motion. Motion meant progress, and that she existed.

Here, the only sound was water and the occasional cry of a seabird that sounded vaguely accusatory.

She glanced at the schedule again. Six thirty. Hydration and Journaling. She had seventeen minutes to achieve inner peace before moving to the next block.

Her phone sat on the wicker table beside her, face down. She'd promised Dr. Smith she wouldn't check work email. She'd promised the HR director the same thing when he'd handed her the sabbatical paperwork with that practiced expression of concern that barely masked his relief at getting her out of the office.

"Two months," he'd said. "Fully paid. Come back refreshed."

What he'd meant was come back fixed or don't come back at all.

She picked up the phone.

Just one look. Just to make sure nothing was on fire. She'd built the Sampson campaign from scratch. She'd landed the pharma account after nine months of pitching. Her team needed her. They had to need her.

She opened her email.

Forty-three unread messages. She scrolled past the newsletters and the automated reports. Nothing urgent. Nothing with her name in the subject line. Nothing that even suggested anyone had noticed her absence beyond the auto-reply she'd been forced to set up.

Then she saw it.

From: Steve Hodges Subject: Weekly Recap. All Good!

Her jaw clenched. She opened it.

Hey team! Quick update on accounts. The Sampson campaign launched successfully (minor tweaks to Cassidy's original plan, but we're tracking above projections). Pharma contract signed this morning. They loved the pitch. Thanks for the foundation work, Cass, wherever you are! Beach treating you well? Don't worry about a thing. Honestly, we've hit our stride. Barely even notice you're gone.

She read it again. *Barely even notice you're gone.*

Her heart rate spiked. The watch buzzed a warning. She dismissed it.

Steve had taken her account. Steve, who'd spent three years riding her coattails and taking credit for her late nights. Steve, who smiled in meetings and undermined her in emails, was apparently thriving in her absence.

She wasn't relieved. She was erased.

The screen blurred. She blinked hard. She was not going to cry over Steve Hodges's passive-aggressive emoji.

She closed the email, deleted it, then pulled it back from trash and marked it unread so she could delete it again later with more intention.

The sunrise had finished happening without her. The sky was fully light now. She'd missed her window for therapeutic reflection.

As she stood, the wicker chair scraped against the wooden deck. She couldn't sit here. If she sat here, she'd open her laptop. If she opened her laptop, she'd start working. If she started working, she'd prove Dr. Smith right about her inability to disengage.

She went inside and paced the small main room, taking in details she'd been too numb to notice when she'd arrived late last night. There were whitewashed walls, pale blue curtains, and a bookshelf stocked with weathered paperbacks and seashells. A vase of fresh wildflowers sat on the counter. The kind of place that showed up in vacation rental listings under tags like *cozy and charming* or *escape the everyday grind.*

She felt like she'd been stuffed into someone else's vision of peace.

The sunroom off the main room made it worse. Winnie Lockhart—her landlord, the lighthouse keeper, the woman who'd greeted her last night with warm eyes and zero questions—had mentioned it when she'd handed over the keys. "Lots of natural light in there. Some of our guests like to write, paint, or knit. It's a good space for thinking."

She had nodded politely and hadn't looked inside.

She looked now.

Floor-to-ceiling windows faced east, washing the room in soft morning sun. Bookshelves lined the far wall. A cozy chair rested beside the windows, begging someone to come sit. She didn't.

It looked like the kind of place where people came to find themselves…

She needed coffee. She needed to be around people. Even strangers. Even small-town strangers who probably moved at half speed and said things like "bless your heart" without irony.

She pulled the sunroom door shut and headed

to the bedroom. Her suitcase sat open on the bedroom floor. She hadn't unpacked because unpacking felt like commitment.

She'd bought new clothes for this trip. Resort wear. Flowy linen pants in cream and soft pink. Loose cotton tops. A straw hat that the sales associate had promised was very beachwear chic.

She ignored all that and pulled out her charcoal blazer. It was sleeveless, structured, with sharp shoulders that meant business. She paired it with tailored black trousers that she'd had hemmed to exact specifications and leather wedges that cost more than most people's monthly car payments.

She dressed with precision. Each piece was armor. Each button was a declaration. There was no reason she couldn't just look like her normal self, was there?

The bathroom mirror was already fogging from humidity despite the air conditioning. She applied her makeup with the same focus she used for client presentations. First concealer, then foundation and a thin line of eyeliner. She finished with red lipstick that said *I am not here to make friends.*

Her hair was another battle. She'd had it cut into a sleek, angled, grazing-her-shoulders bob specifically because it required minimal maintenance. Wash. Blow dry. Flat iron. Done.

Except the Gulf Coast humidity had other plans.

She ran the flat iron over each section twice. The moment she stepped away from the mirror, the ends began to curl in tiny rebellions against her control. She unplugged it and headed out into the main room.

A knock at the door startled her badly enough that she flinched.

"Morning! It's Winnie. I've got muffins if you're interested. No pressure."

Cassidy opened the door because refusing would require explanation. Winnie Lockhart stood on the small porch holding a basket covered with a blue-checked cloth. She was wearing jeans and a cotton shirt like someone who'd never worried about a dress code in her life. Her smile was kind without being invasive.

"Saw you out on your balcony earlier." Winnie held up the basket. "Blueberry. Thought you might like some."

"That's—yes. Thank you." She accepted the basket awkwardly. "You didn't have to."

"I know. I wanted to." Winnie's gaze was steady, assessing without judgment. "Sleep okay?"

"Fine."

A lie, but a polite one. Winnie didn't push.

"Good. Well, I won't keep you. Just wanted to say welcome properly and let you know that if you need anything, I'm just up at the main house."

Winnie left, and Cassidy stood in the doorway

holding a basket of muffins, watching the older woman walk the path back toward the lighthouse with the kind of unhurried grace that came from never having to prove anything to anyone.

She thought of her mother, who moved the same way. She had stayed in the same small Indiana town her whole life, raised two kids, worked part-time at the library, and seemed perfectly content with a life that had never included a corner office, a six-figure salary, or a business card with *Senior Vice President* under her name.

Cassidy had spent her entire adult life making sure she would never become her mother.

And now here she was. Sidelined, exiled, and holding muffins in a cottage by the sea like some kind of recuperating Victorian invalid. She set down the basket and grabbed her phone and wallet.

She did not grab the journal Dr. Smith had recommended. She did not grab the novel that three different people had told her she must read.

She locked the cottage door behind her and started walking.

CHAPTER 2

The path from the lighthouse cottages into town was crushed shell and sand. It was picturesque and probably photographed daily by tourists who thought it was charming.

She walked like she was late for a meeting.

Her wedges sank with each step. The shells crunched and shifted. She had to adjust her pace to keep from twisting an ankle. This was why cities had sidewalks. Sidewalks were efficient and didn't fight back.

The morning air was already thick. She could feel sweat forming at her hairline. Her blazer was a mistake. Everything about this place was a mistake.

A pelican dove into the water near the shore. The splash was enormous and startled her. She was used to pigeons that scattered when you walked past, not prehistoric-looking birds that could probably carry off a small dog.

She kept walking.

The town emerged gradually. First, a bait shop with a hand-painted sign that said "Captain Roy's - Open When We're Here." It was seven in the morning, and the lights were off.

You're missing the morning demographic. Fishermen are up before dawn. This is poor customer service.

She passed a faded wooden sign that said "Welcome to Starlight Shores - A Small Town with a Big Heart." The paint was peeling. The post leaned slightly to the left. Someone had stapled festival flyers to it at random angles. No consistent branding. No clear call to action.

She pulled one off to examine it.

Annual Harbor Festival - July 12-14

Boat Parade! Fresh Seafood! Local Art!

Come Celebrate Our Heritage

The clip art lighthouse looked like it had been downloaded from a free website in 1997. The text was in three different fonts. There was no website listed, no social media handles, just a phone number for more information.

She folded the flyer and put it in her blazer pocket. She wasn't sure why. Professional habit, maybe. The instinct to identify problems even when they weren't hers to solve.

The main street opened up ahead. It ran

parallel to the waterfront, with a post office, a general store with a faded sign reading Bayview, a bookstore called Tides & Tales, and a coffee shop with outdoor tables and a chalkboard menu. Everything was painted in soft pastels with shades of seafoam green, pale coral, and light blue, as if the whole place had agreed on a weathered color palette and stuck to it.

She passed a small gallery with local art in the window and a restaurant with a wooden sign shaped like a sandpiper.

Tourists wandered in couples and families, sunburned and relaxed. Others—locals, she assumed—stopped to chat on corners and waved to each other across the street.

It was aggressively charming. She felt like an anthropologist observing a foreign culture.

She checked her watch. She'd made the walk in twelve minutes. The cottage rental information had said it was a leisurely twenty-minute stroll into town.

She'd saved eight minutes. The small victory felt hollow.

She ended up at the coffee shop, Harbor Brew, because caffeine was non-negotiable and she hadn't thought to check if the cottage had a coffee maker. Through the glass, she could see people moving inside. Real people. Potential witnesses to her continued existence.

She stopped at the door, straightened her blazer,

and checked her reflection in the window. The humidity had already won the battle with her hair. Fine. She'd deal with it.

She pulled the door open.

The air conditioning hit her first. Then the smell of coffee. Dark roast. The good kind. The kind that meant someone here took caffeine seriously.

The space was bigger than it looked from the outside. Exposed brick walls. Mismatched furniture that was probably called eclectic instead of we-couldn't-afford-a-matching-set. Nautical decor that walked the line between charming and excessive. There was a ship's wheel on one wall and vintage photos of fishing boats on another. A large chalkboard menu with actual chalk handwriting hung behind the counter.

People sat scattered at different tables. An elderly man was reading a newspaper. Two women huddled over coffee cups, deep in conversation. They all looked up when she entered.

The assessment was immediate. Her blazer, shoes, and her whole vibe screamed outsider.

The man went back to his newspaper. The women kept staring.

She walked to the counter. A woman with a name tag that said "Jan" looked up from the coffee machine.

"Good morning! You must be new in town." Jan's smile was genuine.

"Just visiting. I need a large coffee. Dark roast. Black."

"You got it. For here or to go?"

"Um…"

"No problem. I'll pour a mug and give you a to-go cup if you decide to finish up later." Jan reached for a large mug. "Staying long?"

The question was casual and friendly. It was the kind of small talk that she normally deflected with professional ease. "Not sure."

"You staying at the lighthouse cottages? I heard Winnie rented out Heron Cottage."

Small towns. Everyone knew everything.

"Yes."

"Oh, you'll love it there. Winnie's the best, and the cottages are so cozy. My cousin got married in that courtyard last spring."

Jan handed over a mug and a to-go cup. "Here you go. You need anything else? Recommendations? We've got the best sunsets on this coast. And if you like seafood, The Sandpiper is right on the water. Best grouper sandwich you'll ever have."

"I'll keep that in mind."

She took the coffee and went over to a table by the window. She sat alone and sipped her coffee.

A woman slid into the chair across from her without asking, and Cassidy looked up, startled.

"Sorry, hope you don't mind," the woman said, though she didn't look sorry. She was older—

seventy, maybe—with short gray hair. "Jan said you were Winnie's new guest. Just wanted to say hi."

Cassidy minded, but saying so felt unnecessarily rude. "It's fine."

"I'm Sally Morris." She stuck out a hand.

She shook it briefly. "Cassidy."

"You're in Heron Cottage, right? Cute cottage. Cliff, have you met him? He's Winnie's nephew and does maintenance around the cottages. He keeps saying he's going to paint it. Last I noticed, it was in need of a bit of a refresh."

She reeled slightly from the deluge of words. "Does everyone in this town know everything immediately?"

Sally grinned. "Pretty much. Don't worry, they'll get bored of you in a week or two." She pulled out her phone and checked a message. "You here for work, or...?"

"Not exactly."

"Vacation?"

"Something like that."

Sally glanced up, assessing, then shrugged. "It's okay. Half the people who stay at the lighthouse are running from something. Winnie's good at giving people space to figure things out."

"I'm not running."

Sally just nodded, stood, and grabbed her coffee. "Well, just wanted to welcome you. If you need a friendly face, I'm always at Bayview General Store. I own it. Feels like I rarely leave it."

She left before Cassidy could respond.

She sat alone again, staring into her coffee.

I'm not running.

But she wasn't staying, either. She was... paused. She was sidelined and waiting for clearance to return to her real life.

This wasn't her life. This was a placeholder.

The two women were still watching her. One leaned over and whispered something to the other. They both smiled.

She dumped what was left of her coffee into the to-go cup before anyone else could ask her questions or stare at her.

She pushed through the door and back into the humidity.

She stood on the sidewalk and looked down the street. The sun was fully up now. The town was waking up. A truck rumbled past. Someone called out a greeting to someone else.

She should go back to the cottage. She should journal. She should do the things Dr. Smith said would help her reconnect with her authentic self. Whatever that meant.

Instead, she walked toward the water.

The harbor opened up at the end of the street. Boats bobbed in their slips. The smell of fish and diesel fuel mixed together. Pelicans perched on the pier posts. A man in waders was hosing down the deck of a fishing boat.

She stopped at the edge of the wharf. The festival flyer crinkled in her pocket. She pulled it out again and studied it. Studied the poor design, lack of strategy, and the missed opportunities.

This isn't your problem.

But her fingers were already itching to open her notes app, sketch out a better approach, and fix what was clearly broken.

She took a sip of coffee and watched the boats. The sun warmed her face.

Two months. Sixty days. Eighty-six thousand four hundred minutes of forced stillness while Steve Hodges took over her life.

She couldn't do it. She couldn't sit on that balcony and pretend she was fine with being erased.

Then she looked at the festival flyer one more time.

She'd finish her coffee and go back to the cottage. She'd change into something more practical.

Her watch buzzed. Eight-thirty. Time for her scheduled power walk.

She looked down at her wedges and the crushed shell path. The oppressive humidity was currently turning her hair into a science experiment.

A seagull landed on a nearby piling and fixed her with one unblinking eye. She stared back.

"What?" she said aloud.

The bird didn't answer. It probably had better things to do than judge her life choices.

CHAPTER 3

Cassidy woke up the next morning to sunlight streaming through the cottage windows and the disorienting sensation of having nowhere to be.

No morning meeting and no inbox full of overnight emails from the London office. No carefully timed coffee run between back-to-back calls.

Just silence and the faint sound of waves.

She lay in bed for three minutes, staring at the ceiling, before the stillness became unbearable.

By seven-thirty, she was dressed—shorts and a linen shirt, the most casual outfit she'd packed—and headed into town. If she had to sit in the cottage for another hour with nothing but her thoughts, she'd lose her mind.

Harbor Brew was busier than it had been yesterday. The tables outside were full, and inside, a line snaked back from the counter. Jan moved behind the counter, calling out orders and chatting with regulars like she had all the time in the world.

Cassidy joined the line and pulled out her phone. No new emails. She refreshed anyway. Still nothing.

She put the phone away and studied the chalkboard menu. When she finally got her order, she headed to an empty table.

She almost laughed as she settled into her seat and looked up. The Wi-Fi password at Harbor Brew was handwritten on a chalkboard: LOCALFIRST.

She stared at the password again, then typed it with more force than necessary. The tablet connected. She opened her email.

The first message was from Steve, sent to the entire team: *Great news! The Riverside account just renewed—18% increase! Thanks for trusting me with this one.*

Her account. Her strategy. Her client relationship.

The second email was worse. HR, following up on her wellness goals for the sabbatical: *Remember, Cassidy, the objective is complete disconnection from work. We're confident the team can handle things in your absence.*

She closed the tablet before she threw it. This town seemed to always make her want to throw her tablet.

A cinnamon roll sat untouched on a small plate,

and she stared out the window. An older man stopped to help a woman load groceries into her car. Two kids chased each other down the sidewalk, laughing. A dog dozed in a patch of sun outside the bookstore.

It was... fine. Pleasant. Unobjectionable.

"More coffee, hon?" Jan appeared with the pot, already refilling Cassidy's cup before she could answer. The woman had sun-weathered skin and the kind of easy smile that suggested she'd never spent a single night worrying about quarterly projections.

"Thanks." She wrapped both hands around the mug. The ceramic was thick, warm, and nothing like the paper cups she usually clutched during conference calls.

"You settling in okay at the lighthouse?" Jan set the pot on the table and leaned against the chair across from Cassidy, not asking permission, just claiming space.

"It's quiet."

"That's kind of the point." Jan's smile widened. "Winnie's got good instincts about who needs what. She put you in Heron Cottage, right? That one's got the best view of the sunrise."

"I wouldn't know. I'm not really a morning person." Sure, she was. Why had she said that?

Jan straightened, retrieving the coffee pot. "Well, let me know if you need anything."

She was gone before Cassidy could explain that she didn't need anything except for her real life back.

The bell over the door jangled. Four women entered in a cluster, laughing about something one of them had said outside on the sidewalk. They were in their late sixties, maybe early seventies, and dressed in casual beach clothes that somehow looked both comfortable and coordinated. They moved with the confidence of people who owned their space.

Jan didn't take their order. She just brought a pot of coffee and four cups to their usual corner table.

She watched them settle in. She'd done enough market research to recognize a demographic when she saw one. Female, retirement age, fixed income, high community engagement. The kind of customers who'd rather complain about change than adapt to it.

"The festival committee is meeting again soon." The woman with short gray hair—Donna, based on how the others addressed her—sounded irritated. "I don't know why the mayor keeps pushing for fresh ideas. We've done it the same way for thirty years."

"Because attendance was down last year." Another woman, thin and softer-spoken. "And the year before. We need something, Donna."

"We need people to appreciate tradition, not chase after Instagram-y nonsense."

Cassidy's attention sharpened. Were they talking about the same festival from the flyer she'd picked up yesterday?

A festival with declining attendance and a resistance to innovation. This was a problem she could solve in her sleep.

Not your problem, she reminded herself. *You're here to rest and disconnect.*

She picked up the cinnamon roll and took a bite. It was still warm, sticky with icing, and better than it had any right to be.

A woman entered like she owned the place. A man followed in her wake, looking like he didn't really want to be there. They ordered and sat at a table near the window.

She couldn't help overhearing their conversation.

"—can't keep pretending it's fine. Last year's crowd was the lowest we've had in a decade."

She glanced over.

The woman sat across from the man, her posture tense despite the casual setting. She had short silver hair, sharp eyes, and the kind of presence that suggested she was used to being listened to. A leather portfolio sat open on the table between them, pages of notes visible.

"I know the numbers," the man said. He

sounded tired. "But what do you want me to do? We've tried posters, we've tried social media—"

"Posters," the woman repeated, flat. "Marty, we're trying to save a festival with *posters*."

"We don't have the budget for anything else."

"Then we find the budget. Or we find someone who knows how to do more with less." She tapped the portfolio with one finger. "If we can't turn this around, we're not just losing the festival. We're losing the tourists who come for it, the weekend foot traffic, and the restaurant bookings. Do you know what that does to the waterfront businesses?"

She told herself, again, to stop listening. This wasn't her problem.

"I know," the man said quietly. "But unless you've got a marketing firm willing to work for free—"

"We don't need a firm. We need one person who can think beyond what we've always done." The woman sat back, frustration visible. "This town can't afford to be seen as just another dying small town. We need to prove we're still worth visiting."

Cassidy's fingers twitched toward her phone. She could sketch a preliminary audit in her head already: identify target demographics, assess current brand perception, build a tiered engagement strategy with measurable—

She stopped herself. She should go. She

gathered her wallet and tablet and stood. She made it three steps before her mouth betrayed her.

"Excuse me."

The woman at the table looked up, eyebrows raised.

She paused, already regretting it. "I'm sorry, I overheard you talking about the festival. If you're looking at audience engagement strategies, you might want to segment your messaging by visitor type. Families, couples, locals—they all respond to different value propositions. Posters are fine for broad awareness, but if you're trying to drive attendance, you need targeted digital campaigns with clear CTAs—um, calls to action."

The woman blinked. Then she smiled, slow and assessing. "And you are?"

"Cassidy Wren. I'm—" She hesitated. "I'm staying at the lighthouse cottages."

"Linda West. I'm the mayor." She gestured to the man across from her. "This is Marty Fuller. He runs Tides & Tales Bookshop and is on the festival committee."

Marty nodded, looking wary. "You work in marketing?"

"I'm a marketing executive." She paused. "Or I was."

"Was?" The mayor's gaze sharpened.

"I'm on a bit of a break."

The mayor leaned back in her chair, studying

her. "Have you ever handled something like this? A local event, limited budget, declining attendance?"

"Not exactly. My background is in corporate brand strategy and product launches. But the principles are the same. You're selling an experience. You need to understand your audience and build a conversion funnel that moves people from awareness to action."

Marty exchanged a glance with Linda. "All those fancy terms sound expensive."

"It doesn't have to be. You'd be surprised what you can do with good messaging and a few strategic partnerships."

The mayor set down her pen. "How long are you in town?"

"I don't know yet." Well, yes, she did. Two months. Two forced months.

"Would you be willing to consult? Even informally. We could use a fresh perspective."

"I—" Cassidy stopped. "I'm not really here to work."

"I'm not asking you to run the whole thing. Just give us some advice. Maybe sit in on a planning meeting. You've already given me more useful direction in two minutes than I've gotten in the last six months."

The door to the coffee shop opened, and Winnie stepped inside.

She spotted Cassidy immediately, smiled, and

walked over. "Morning. I thought I might find you here."

"Winnie," the mayor said warmly. "Perfect timing. I'm trying to recruit your guest."

Winnie raised an eyebrow. "For what?"

"The festival. She's got a marketing background, and we're desperate."

Winnie looked at Cassidy, her expression thoughtful. "Is that right?"

"I just made a comment," she said quickly. "I wasn't offering to—"

"She suggested audience segmentation and targeted digital campaigns," the mayor said. "In about thirty seconds, she identified half the problems we've been ignoring."

Winnie's smile softened. "That sounds promising. Sounds like you know how to fix things."

"I appreciate the offer," she said carefully, "but I'm really not in a position to take on a project."

"It wouldn't have to be a big commitment," the mayor added. "Just a few hours here and there. You'd be doing the town a real favor."

"I'm sure you'll figure it out."

The mayor didn't push, but her expression made it clear she wasn't giving up. "Well, if you change your mind, let me know. Here, let me put my number in your phone."

She reluctantly handed over her phone. The mayor typed in her number and sent her a message.

"So, you'll have my phone number too," the mayor said as she handed back the phone.

Cassidy nodded and turned toward the door. Winnie followed her out.

They walked in silence for half a block before Winnie spoke. "You didn't have to say no."

"I'm on vacation. I'm supposed to be resting."

"Resting doesn't mean doing nothing."

Cassidy stopped walking and turned to face her. "I can't take on someone else's problem right now. I have enough of my own."

Winnie met her gaze, calm and steady. "Sometimes working on someone else's problem is easier than sitting alone with your own."

"That's avoidance."

"Maybe. Or maybe it's a way to remember what you're good at while you figure out what comes next."

She looked away. "I don't know what comes next."

"That's okay." Winnie's voice was gentle. "You don't have to know yet. You just have to take the next step."

"And you think the next step is running a small-town festival?"

"I think the next step is whatever keeps you from disappearing into that cottage and mulling over your problems."

She opened her mouth to argue, then closed it.

Winnie touched her arm briefly. "You don't have to decide now. Just think about it."

She walked away, leaving Cassidy standing on the sidewalk with the uncomfortable sensation that Winnie saw straight through her.

Cassidy spent the rest of the morning walking the town, this time with a different lens.

She noticed things she'd missed before, like the faded paint on the dress shop sign and the empty storefronts at the south end of Main Street. The tourist families who wandered through quickly, bought ice cream, and left.

No one stayed long.

There was no reason to.

She found herself standing in front of a community bulletin board outside the post office, scanning the flyers.

Harbor Festival – July 12-14

Lighthouse Tours • Local Vendors • Live Music

Family Fun on the Waterfront!

Similar to the flyer she'd seen yesterday. The design was dated, with no clear call to action and no sense of what made this festival different from any other small-town summer event.

She pulled out her phone and took a picture.

Then she put the phone away, annoyed with herself.

This was not her problem. How many times did

she have to repeat that? And hadn't she just turned down the mayor?

She walked back to the cottage and sat at the table with her laptop.

Opened a blank document.

Stared at it, then typed: Starlight Harbor Festival. A Preliminary Assessment.

She stared at that, then deleted it and closed the laptop.

Her phone buzzed with a message from her mom: *How are you doing? Maybe you should come home for a bit.*

Home.

A town smaller than this one. A house that still had her high school photos on the wall. A mother who'd never understood why Cassidy worked sixty-hour weeks, why she couldn't just relax, why she needed the promotions, recognition, and the proof that she was worth something.

She had left at eighteen and never looked back.

And now she was forty-two, sitting in a cottage a thousand miles from her apartment, with no job to go to and no idea who she was if she wasn't the woman who delivered results, exceeded expectations, and made things happen.

Well, she sure wasn't going home, that was for sure.

She opened her phone, pulled up the photo of

the festival flyer, then spread out the paper flyer she'd picked up yesterday.

She could do this. A basic audit, just to see what they were working with. It wouldn't take more than an hour. She wouldn't commit to anything. She'd just... look.

She opened the laptop again and started typing. By the time the sun started to set, she had three pages of notes.

Target audience profiles. Messaging frameworks. Partnership opportunities. A rough content calendar for a six-week pre-event campaign.

She sat back and looked at the screen.

This was what she did. What she was good at. She took something broken and figured out how to make it work.

Her phone buzzed with a text from the mayor: *No pressure, but if you want to sit in on our next planning meeting, it's Thursday at 10. Bayview General Store back room. Coffee's on me.*

She stared at the message.

She should say no. She should delete it and go back to doing whatever people on mandatory sabbaticals were supposed to do.

But the document on her screen was the first thing she'd felt even remotely competent doing since HR had forced a sabbatical on her.

Winnie's words about working on someone else's

problem being easier than sitting with your own kept echoing in her head.

She typed a reply: *I'll think about it.*

Sent it before she could change her mind.

Then she closed the laptop, walked to the sunroom door, and opened it.

The light was fading and washed the room in soft gold. The chair by the window looked inviting. The bookshelves were full of titles she didn't recognize.

It still felt like someone else's space, but maybe that was the point. A new space.

She stepped inside, sat in the chair, and looked out at the water.

CHAPTER 4

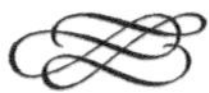

The Bayview General Store smelled like old wood and coffee. Cassidy stood just inside the entrance on Thursday morning, ten minutes early, scanning the space for a back room that wasn't immediately obvious.

The store itself was a cluttered maze of practical goods: canned food, fishing tackle, sunscreen, and beach towels with dolphins on them. A refrigerator case hummed near the counter, and postcards spun on a wire rack by the window.

Sally Morris looked up from behind the register. "You came."

"I told the mayor I'd think about it."

"And you thought about it." Sally's grin was knowing. "Back room's through there." She pointed toward a doorway half-hidden behind a display of pool noodles. "Coffee's already on. Mayor got here twenty minutes ago. She's been pacing."

She nodded and made her way through the store, weaving between shelves that seemed designed to maximize confusion. The back room, when she found it, was surprisingly spacious. A long table was surrounded by mismatched chairs. A whiteboard hung on one wall, covered in faded marker, and a window looked out onto a small parking lot.

Mayor West sat at the head of the table, a legal pad in front of her covered in notes. Marty Fuller was there too, nursing a cup of coffee and looking like he'd rather be anywhere else. Two other people Cassidy didn't recognize occupied chairs near the middle, a younger woman and an older man with weathered hands and a skeptical expression.

And at the far end of the table, arms crossed, sat a man who looked at her like she'd just tracked mud across his floor.

"Cassidy." The mayor stood, gesturing to an empty chair. "Glad you could make it. Everyone, this is Cassidy Wren. She's staying at the lighthouse and has some experience in marketing. She's agreed to sit in and offer a fresh perspective."

"I haven't agreed to anything. I'm just here to listen." But she sat anyway.

The man at the end of the table made a sound that might have been a laugh. "Fresh perspective.

That's what we need. Someone from out of town to tell us how to run our own festival."

"Bryan." The mayor's voice carried a warning.

"What? I'm just saying what everyone's thinking." He unfolded his arms and leaned forward. "No offense, but we've had consultants before. They come in, throw around buzzwords, charge a fortune, and leave us with a plan that doesn't fit who we are."

She met his gaze. "I'm not a consultant. And I'm not charging anything."

"Then what are you?"

"Someone who overheard a conversation and made the mistake of opening her mouth."

The young woman snorted. The older man's expression didn't change.

"Bryan is the festival committee head," the mayor explained.

Great, just great.

Bryan studied her for a moment. He was maybe her age, early forties, with dark hair going gray at the temples and the kind of tan that came from years of outdoor work rather than beach vacations. His eyes were sharp and assessing.

"Fair enough," he said finally. "But if you're just here to listen, then listen. Don't tell us what we're doing wrong until you understand what we're trying to do."

"That seems reasonable."

The mayor cleared her throat. "Good. Now that we've established ground rules, can we actually start the meeting?"

For the next forty minutes, Cassidy listened.

She learned that the Starlight Harbor Festival had been running for seventy-four years. That it used to draw crowds from all over the Gulf Coast —families, day-trippers, people who came for the lighthouse tours and stayed for the food and music. That attendance had peaked about fifteen years ago and had been declining steadily ever since.

She learned that the budget was tight. They relied on local sponsors who were increasingly reluctant to commit. The committee was made up of volunteers who had other jobs and other lives and couldn't devote the hours needed to do real outreach.

She learned that Bryan cared deeply about authenticity, and he'd grown up coming to this festival with his parents. His family's restaurant had been a vendor since the beginning, and he saw the event as more than just a tourism draw. It was a piece of the town's identity.

And she suspected he was terrified of losing it.

Not that he said so. But she could hear it in the way he talked about preserving what made the town special. His resistance wasn't stubbornness. It was fear dressed up as principle.

She recognized the strategy. She'd used it herself, once or twice.

When the discussion turned to marketing—or specifically, the lack of it—she couldn't help herself.

"You mentioned social media earlier," she said, interrupting Marty mid-sentence. "What platforms are you using?"

Marty blinked. "We have a Facebook page."

"When was the last time you posted?"

A pause. "March, maybe?"

"It's May."

"We've been busy."

She pulled out her phone and typed quickly. "Your page has four hundred followers. Your last post got twelve likes. Your cover photo is from 2019." She looked up. "You're invisible."

Bryan's jaw tightened. "We're not invisible. People know about the festival."

"People who already live here, maybe. But you said yourself that attendance is down. That means you're not reaching new audiences. And you can't reach new audiences if you're not showing up where they are."

"So what, we need to go viral? Get some influencer to come take pictures and pretend they care about our little town?" He rolled his eyes.

"No. You need to tell a story that makes people want to be part of something." She set her phone down. "Right now, you're not telling any story at all.

You're just existing and hoping people will remember you exist too."

The room went quiet.

The young woman was watching her with interest. The older man was frowning. The mayor looked like she was trying not to smile.

Bryan looked like he was trying not to throw something.

"You've been here five minutes," he said. "And you think you know what we need."

"I've been here five minutes, and I can see what's not working. That's not the same thing. I'm not saying I have all the answers. I'm saying you're not asking the right questions."

"And what questions should we be asking?"

"Who are you trying to reach? What do you want them to feel? Why should they choose this festival over everything else competing for their attention?" She paused. "Until you answer them, no amount of posters or Facebook posts is going to make a difference."

Bryan stared at her.

Then he pushed back his chair and stood. "I need some air."

He walked out of the room without looking back.

The mayor sighed. "Well. That went well."

The meeting limped along for another twenty minutes after Bryan left. Marty took notes. The older man—Frank, the harbormaster, she finally found out—offered a few logistical updates about permits and parking.

She said very little. She'd already said too much.

When the meeting finally ended, she slipped out before anyone could corner her for follow-up conversation. She needed coffee. She needed to walk. She needed to figure out why she'd let herself get pulled into someone else's problem when she'd specifically come here to avoid exactly that.

CHAPTER 5

The afternoon sun beat down on the dock as Bryan stepped out of the harbormaster's office and onto the weathered planks. He'd spent the last two hours listening to Rod Harris from the Coast Guard station explain catch limits, new regulations, and environmental impact studies that might shut down three more fishing routes by next season.

Might as well have been listening to a eulogy.

Bryan walked toward his boat, the *Mary Catherine*, named after his grandmother. The thirty-foot commercial vessel had belonged to his father before him. Before that, his grandfather. Three generations of Lucas men had hauled nets from this deck. Now both his father and grandfather were gone, and it was just him.

He checked the mooring lines out of habit.

Everything was secure. If only the rest of his life had the same guarantee.

"Bryan Lucas?"

The voice came from behind him. Smooth. Professional. The kind of voice that belonged in an office building, not on a working dock.

He turned. A man in a pressed white shirt and khakis stood at the edge of the pier. No tie, but he might as well have been wearing one. Everything about him screamed money and mainland.

"That's me."

The man extended his hand as he approached. "George Morton. I'm with Oceanside Development. Do you have a few minutes?"

Bryan shook his hand because that's what you did, even when every instinct said to walk away. "Depends what you're selling."

Morton smiled. It was the kind of smile that probably worked on investors and city councils. "I'm not selling anything. I'm here to make an offer."

"On what?"

"Your dock rights." Morton pulled a folder from under his arm. "And your restaurant space. We're in the process of acquiring waterfront properties along this section of the harbor for commercial revitalization. Businesses like high-end retail, boutique restaurants, and a resort component."

"The Sandpiper has been in our family for years."

"Of course." Morton's smile didn't waver. "And it's a charming establishment. Very authentic. But we're talking about something that would bring significant revenue to this community. It would bring jobs, tourism, and real economic growth."

Real. As if what he did every day wasn't real work. Fishing. Working in the restaurant.

"My family's been fishing these waters since before you were born. Before your company existed."

"I understand the emotional attachment." Morton opened the folder. "That's why we're prepared to make a very fair offer for your cooperation."

He turned the folder so Bryan could see the number written on the top page.

Bryan looked at it. Looked at Morton. Looked back at the number.

It was insulting. "That's what you think my livelihood is worth?"

"It's a starting point for negotiation. The truth is, Mr. Lucas, the fishing industry is dying. You know it. I know it. This harbor can either evolve or become obsolete."

Bryan's hands clenched at his sides. He wanted to throw Morton off the dock and watch him splash into the water in that pressed white shirt.

But that wasn't how things worked anymore. You couldn't just punch problems in the face and watch them sink.

"I'm not selling," Bryan said.

"I understand you need time to consider." Morton pulled a business card from his pocket. "But I should mention that we're acquiring multiple properties in this area. With or without your cooperation, this waterfront is going to change. The only question is whether you're part of that change or fighting against it."

He held out the card.

Bryan didn't take it.

Morton set it on the dock railing. "Think it over. We'll be in touch." He walked away. His shoes made clean, precise sounds on the planks, like he was already measuring the space for whatever sterile replacement he had planned.

He picked up the business card. Oceanside Development and Acquisition. A phone number. An email address.

He tore it in half. Then tore the halves into smaller pieces. He would have tossed them into the wind, but he didn't litter. He shoved them into his pocket.

The *Mary Catherine* rocked gently in the tide. He climbed aboard and sat on the bench near the helm. His father used to sit here in the evenings, going over the day's catch, mending nets, planning the next morning's run.

Those evenings were gone. The catches were smaller, and the regulations tighter. The profit margins were so thin you could see through them.

Maybe Morton was right. Maybe this was all dying.

He pulled out his phone. Two missed calls from his mother and a text from his sister asking if he'd picked up supplies for the restaurant. Nothing from the bank, which meant his loan extension request was still pending.

He scrolled through his email. Most of it was automated newsletters and spam. An email from Marty Fuller at the bookstore, forwarding an article about heritage tourism. One message from Mayor West thanking the committee for their work today, especially Cassidy Wren for her suggestions.

The mayor had dropped by this afternoon and assured him that Cassidy was just here for advising. He was still the head of the committee. He made the final decisions.

Cassidy Wren. She'd sat there at the meeting with her neat folder, her color-coded tabs, and her corporate confidence. Talked about demographics, marketing funnels—whatever those were—and social media engagement, like the festival was just another product to sell.

Cassidy was exactly like Morton. Maybe she dressed it up in prettier language, called it revitalization instead of development, and used words like authentic and heritage. But at the end of the day, she wanted the same thing Morton wanted.

She wanted to turn Starlight Shores into something shiny and new that looked good in photographs. Something that brought in tourists who'd take their selfies, eat their overpriced fish tacos, and leave without ever understanding what this place actually was.

She saw the festival as a marketing opportunity and the working waterfront as a quaint aesthetic choice. She didn't see the people or the families. The generations of men and women who'd built their lives on these docks.

He stood and checked the fuel gauge. He needed to take the boat out tomorrow. Early. Before the heat set in.

His phone buzzed. Another text from his mother. *Did you talk to the bank?*

He typed back. *Still waiting.*

The sun was starting its descent toward the horizon. Golden light spread across the water. This was usually his favorite time of day. The time when everything felt possible, like the next morning's catch might be the one that changed everything.

But today it just felt heavy.

He looked back toward town. He could see the lighthouse in the distance. Heron Cottage would be beside it, where Cassidy Wren was probably sitting right now, working on her next presentation about how to fix everything that wasn't broken.

Or maybe everything was broken. Maybe he just couldn't see it yet.

Morton's offer sat in his mind like a splinter, painful and persistent.

He checked the boat one last time and headed back down the dock. He had to get to the restaurant. The dinner shift had started an hour ago, and they were down a server. His mother would cover, like she always did, but she shouldn't have to.

None of them should have to work this hard just to keep what was already theirs.

CHAPTER 6

The knock came at nine in the morning, just as Cassidy was finishing her second cup of coffee and staring at her color-coded sabbatical schedule like it might suddenly make sense.

She opened the door to find Mayor West on her porch, looking far too energetic for a Monday morning.

"Cassidy. Good, you're awake." The mayor stepped inside without waiting for an invitation. "I won't take much of your time."

Her instincts kicked in immediately. She recognized a sales pitch when she saw one coming. "Coffee?"

"No, thank you. I'll get right to it." The mayor settled into one of the wicker chairs near the window, her posture straight and purposeful. "I want you to co-chair the festival committee. With Bryan."

The coffee cup paused halfway to her lips. "You want me to what?"

"Co-chair with Bryan Lucas." Mayor West folded her hands in her lap like she'd just proposed something perfectly reasonable. "You'd share the responsibilities. Planning, execution, all of it."

"I gave you some basic marketing advice. That doesn't qualify me to run your festival."

"You had some very good ideas. I'm afraid you're our only hope." The mayor leaned forward. "And Winnie mentioned you'd rented Heron Cottage for two months."

The words sat between them.

"Bryan's already the chair. He doesn't need someone swooping in to take over."

"He needs help. The man works eighteen-hour days between the restaurant and the fishing boat. The festival has suffered because he simply doesn't have the bandwidth. You'd be doing him a favor."

"I'm not sure Bryan would see it that way."

"He's practical. Once he understands the value you bring, he'll come around."

She almost laughed. The man had walked out of the meeting rather than listen to her suggestions, but she kept that observation to herself.

"I'm on sabbatical," she said instead. "Mandatory rest. Doctor's orders."

"This wouldn't be stressful. It's a small-town festival, not a corporate merger." The mayor stood, smoothing her skirt. "Think about it. Bryan's a good man, and he's dedicated to this town. He just needs support. And frankly, you looked animated and alive when you gave us your ideas."

The words landed like a gentle slap. She opened her mouth to argue, but Linda was already moving toward the door.

"I'll tell Bryan you're considering it. We're meeting again on Friday to finalize the budget. That gives you time to decide." She paused at the threshold. "I think you're exactly what this festival needs, Cassidy. What this town needs."

Then she was gone, leaving Cassidy standing in her too-quiet cottage with her color-coded schedule mocking her from the coffee table.

She headed for the courtyard. She needed to move, think, and do something other than stare at the walls of Heron Cottage and feel her career slipping further away with each passing hour.

The courtyard was peaceful in the late morning light. Native plantings framed the pathways, and the bench dedicated to the Lockhart family sat in dappled shade beneath a sprawling live oak. She had walked past it a dozen times but had never really looked at it.

Winnie knelt near one of the flower beds, her hands working the soil. She wore gardening gloves and a wide-brimmed hat that had seen better decades.

"Morning, Cassidy." Winnie sat back on her heels, wiping her forehead with the back of one glove. "How are you settling in?"

"Fine. Good." Cassidy shoved her hands into her pockets. "Mayor West just stopped by."

"Did she now?" Winnie's expression didn't change, but something in her tone suggested she wasn't surprised.

"She wants me to co-chair the festival committee… with Bryan Lucas."

"That sounds like Linda." Winnie pulled a weed free and added it to the small pile beside her. "What did you tell her?"

"That I'd think about it. But I'm pretty sure Bryan would rather eat glass than work with me."

Winnie chuckled softly. "Bryan's stubborn, I'll give you that. But he's not unreasonable."

"He walked out of the meeting when I suggested updating the festival's social media."

"Because he's scared." Winnie looked up, her eyes kind but direct. "That festival is tied to every memory he has of his grandfather. His father. Changing it feels like losing them."

She shifted her weight. "I'm not trying to erase anyone's memories. I'm just trying to help them reach more people."

"I know that. And deep down, Bryan probably

knows it too." Winnie returned her attention to the flower bed. "He works himself half to death trying to keep everything afloat. The restaurant, the fishing business, and the festival. He's terrified he'll be the Lucas who lets it all slip away."

The words settled uncomfortably over her. She understood that fear. The terror of being the one who failed and who wasn't enough.

"The festival committee needs fresh energy," Winnie continued. "And Bryan needs someone who can carry part of the load, whether he admits it or not."

"You think I should do it."

"Linda said you looked happy at that meeting when you were giving your ideas. Engaged." Winnie pulled off her gloves and stood, brushing dirt from her knees. "Even when Bryan was being difficult."

"I was annoyed, not happy."

"Sometimes those feel the same when you've spent too long feeling nothing at all."

The observation hit too close to home. She looked away, focusing on the lighthouse rising beyond the courtyard. The white tower gleamed in the morning sun, solid and permanent in a way nothing in her life had ever felt.

"Bryan's a good man," Winnie said quietly. "He cares deeply about this town and about doing right by the people who came before him. That kind of loyalty is rare."

"I'm not questioning his character. I'm just not sure we can work together."

"Maybe that's exactly why you should try."

Winnie gathered her gardening tools and headed toward the keeper's quarters, leaving Cassidy alone in the courtyard with her tangled thoughts.

Back in Heron Cottage, she tried to focus on anything other than the mayor's offer.

She reorganized her closet with shirts, then slacks, then the few dresses she had brought. By color, of course. She alphabetized the books on the shelf. Made notes about the cottage's decor that absolutely no one had asked for.

By three in the afternoon, she had run out of distractions.

She opened her laptop, telling herself she was just checking email and staying informed. Nothing wrong with that.

Her inbox was a disaster. Forty-seven unread messages, most of them automated newsletters or client updates she would normally scan in seconds. But mixed in among them was one from Steve Hodges with the subject line: "Quick Update."

She gritted her teeth.

Steve had been nipping at her heels for two years, always one step behind but desperate to close the gap. He smiled too widely in meetings and took credit for collaborative ideas like they'd sprung fully formed from his own brilliant mind.

She clicked the message open.

Cassidy,

Hope you're enjoying your time away! Just wanted to keep you in the loop. The Marnetti campaign you started is moving forward. I've taken point on the execution side, and the client is thrilled with the direction. Might be wrapping it up before you're back.

Also, David mentioned he's bringing me into the Phillips pitch meeting next week. Big opportunity. Wish me luck!

Rest up.

Steve

She read it twice.

The Marnetti campaign was hers. She'd spent four months building that strategy and nurturing that client relationship. Now Steve was sliding into her chair like she'd never existed.

The Phillips account was the crown jewel of their division.

Rest up.

Like she was some fragile thing that needed to be handled carefully while the real work got done by people who could handle the pressure.

She'd spent fifteen years building her reputation.

She'd sacrificed sleep, relationships, and any semblance of work-life balance. And two months away—forced months—was all it took for Steve Hodges to start dismantling everything she'd built.

She closed the laptop with a resounding snap.

She grabbed her phone and pulled up Mayor West's number, her thumb hovering over the call button.

This was stupid. Reckless. She was supposed to be resting, not diving headfirst into a high-stakes community project.

But sitting here doing nothing while Steve took over her career felt like dying slowly.

At least the festival would give her something to show for these two months. Something concrete. A portfolio piece that proved she was still sharp and still capable. She was still Cassidy Wren, a marketing executive who could turn around failing projects in her sleep.

She wasn't doing this for Starlight Shores.

She was doing this because Steve Hodges needed to remember exactly who he was dealing with. Anyway, she'd build something here. Maybe, when she got back, she'd even pitch small-town revitalization as a new service vertical. Besides, she'd already proven to herself that she couldn't just sit still, and this felt like work without the baggage.

She sat back. Had she thrown enough

justifications at herself yet? She almost wanted to roll her eyes at herself.

But was this the right thing to do?

She made the call before she could talk herself out of it.

The mayor answered on the second ring. "Cassidy. I was hoping to hear from you."

"I'll do it." The words came out clipped and decisive, more decisive than she felt. "I'll co-chair the festival with Bryan."

"Excellent. I knew you'd come around."

"I have conditions."

"Of course you do." The mayor sounded amused. "Go ahead."

"I need full access to all previous festival records. Marketing materials, budgets, attendance data. Everything."

"Done."

"And I need authority to implement necessary changes. I'm not interested in co-chairing if it means every decision requires a committee vote."

There was a pause. "Bryan will need to sign off on major changes. It's his committee."

"Then make sure Bryan understands that I'm there to help, not to take over." She paced the length of the cottage, her professional instincts kicking into high gear. "I'll respect his knowledge of the community, but he needs to respect my expertise."

"I'll talk to him this afternoon."

"When's the next meeting?"

"Friday afternoon. Two o'clock at the store."

"I'll be there." She stopped at the window overlooking the courtyard. The lighthouse stood tall in her peripheral vision, its white walls almost glowing in the afternoon light. "And Mayor? I'm not doing this as a favor. I expect this to be a legitimate professional engagement. Portfolio-worthy."

"You'll have my full support." The mayor's voice softened slightly. "Thank you, Cassidy. This means more to the town than you realize."

She ended the call and set her phone down carefully. Her heart raced. The familiar buzz of a new project hummed through her, washing away the restless anxiety that had plagued her since arriving in Starlight Shores.

She opened her laptop again and created a new folder: Starlight Harbor Festival.

Then she began drafting a preliminary timeline. Six weeks until the festival wasn't much time. She'd need to assess the current marketing strategy, identify quick wins, and develop a comprehensive plan that balanced authenticity with broader appeal.

Her fingers flew across the keyboard. This was what she was good at. This was who she was.

Steve Hodges could have the Marnetti campaign. She'd create something better right here in this tiny coastal town, and when she returned to the office, she'd have proof that Cassidy Wren was still the best in the business.

She worked through dinner, only stopping when her stomach growled loud enough to break her concentration. The sun had set while she worked, and the lighthouse beam swept across the water in its steady rotation.

She grabbed a granola bar from the kitchen and returned to her laptop.

She was drafting a sponsor outreach strategy when a small voice in the back of her mind whispered that she'd just done exactly what her therapist had warned her not to do. She had jumped back into work and found a new project to obsess over. She was avoiding the actual rest and reflection she was supposed to be doing.

She told that voice to shut up.

This was different. The festival was helping a community and supporting local businesses. That was meaningful work, not just corporate ladder climbing, right?

The next morning, Cassidy woke early and dressed in cream linen pants and a navy blouse. Professional but approachable. She tied a silk scarf around her neck and studied her reflection in the mirror.

She looked like someone in control. Someone who knew what she was doing.

She made coffee and opened her laptop to continue her planning but found herself distracted by the view from the cottage windows. The morning light illuminated the lighthouse, and the water beyond sparkled like scattered diamonds.

It was beautiful. There was no denying that.

She wondered if Bryan saw it that way. If he looked at this view and saw beauty or just the weight of generations depending on him to keep it all from disappearing.

The thought annoyed her. She didn't need to understand Bryan Lucas. She just needed to work with him long enough to turn the festival into a success.

Then she could go back to her real life, her real career.

This was just a detour, a portfolio piece, and nothing more.

She closed the laptop and carried her coffee out to the courtyard.

Winnie was already there, watering the flower beds with an old metal watering can.

"You're up early," the older woman observed.

"Productive morning." Cassidy sipped her coffee. "I called Mayor West yesterday and told her I'd co-chair the festival."

Winnie's face broke into a warm smile. "That's wonderful. Bryan will come around. You'll see."

"I'm not doing it for Bryan." The words were a little too sharp. She tried again. "I'm doing it because I need a project. Something to work on."

"Whatever gets you there." Winnie moved to the next flower bed, her movements unhurried. "The festival's lucky to have you."

She wanted to argue and explain that this was strategic, that she was using Starlight Shores as much as they were using her.

But Winnie had already moved on, humming softly as she tended the plants. The lighthouse stood quiet and watchful over the courtyard.

She finished her coffee and headed back inside. She had work to do.

Steve Hodges had no idea what was coming. Neither did Bryan Lucas. She'd prove them both wrong.

CHAPTER 7

Cassidy arrived at the Bayview General Store conference room fifteen minutes early. She balanced a leather portfolio, her laptop, and a canvas tote bag filled with printed copies of her presentation. The morning air was already thick with humidity, and she'd made the mistake of wearing a silk blouse. It clung to her back as she pushed through the door.

She set up her laptop and began arranging handouts at each seat. The presentation had taken her until two in the morning to finish, but it was good. Really good. Color-coded timelines, budget breakdowns, sponsor outreach templates, and social media calendars. Everything they needed to turn the festival around.

She smoothed her skirt and checked her watch. Ten minutes.

The door swung open. Sally Morris entered first, carrying a box of pastries. "Morning, dear. I brought bear claws."

"That's thoughtful. Thank you." Cassidy gestured to the table. "I've prepared materials for everyone."

Sally picked up a handout and flipped through it. Her eyebrows rose. "Well. You've been busy."

Mayor West arrived next, followed by Marty Fuller. They settled into their seats and reached for the materials. Bryan came in last. He wore a faded shirt with the sleeves rolled up and jeans that had seen better days. He glanced at Cassidy's setup, then took the seat farthest from her.

"Good morning, everyone." Mayor West smiled brightly. "Cassidy has put together something to share with us today."

"I can see that." Bryan picked up his copy of the handout, but he didn't open it.

She stood and opened her laptop. The projector hummed to life. "I've spent the last few days analyzing the festival's historical performance data and comparing it to similar events in coastal communities. What I've found is that we have significant opportunities for growth, but we need to approach this strategically."

She clicked to the first slide. It showed a graph tracking attendance over the past decade. "As you can see, attendance has declined by thirty-eight percent since 2015. However, that's actually on par with similar events that haven't adapted their marketing approach."

Bryan leaned back in his chair, arms crossed over his chest.

"The good news is that coastal tourism in Florida is actually up. We're not losing visitors because people don't want to come to places like Starlight Shores. We're losing them because they don't know we exist." She clicked to the next slide. "Here's our current digital footprint."

The screen showed their barely active Facebook page, the lack of an Instagram presence, and a website that looked like it hadn't been updated since 2010.

Sally winced. "Oh my."

"It's not great," Cassidy agreed. "But it's fixable. What we need is a comprehensive digital strategy that reaches our target demographics where they actually spend their time." She clicked through slides showing sample social media posts, influencer partnership opportunities, and targeted ad campaigns.

"Now, I've broken down the action items into phases." She distributed a second handout. This one was a detailed timeline spanning the next six weeks. "Phase one focuses on establishing our digital presence and creating shareable content. Phase two is about partnership development and sponsor outreach. Phase three is the final push with coordinated advertising and media coverage."

Marty studied the timeline. "This is thorough."

"Thank you. I've also included budget estimates for each phase. Some of this we can do for free using existing platforms and community volunteers. The paid advertising component would require an investment of approximately five thousand dollars, but I believe we could secure local business sponsorships to cover most of that cost."

She clicked to another slide. "I've identified twelve potential sponsors who align with our target demographics. Here's a draft sponsorship package with tiered benefits."

Mayor West leaned forward. "Cassidy, this is impressive."

Bryan's chair scraped against the floor. "Can I say something?"

"Of course." She paused the presentation. "I'm open to feedback."

"This isn't the Starlight Harbor Festival." He tapped the handout. "This is some corporate marketing campaign that could be for any event in any town."

Heat flushed her face. "I'm not sure what you mean. Everything here is specifically tailored to this community."

"Really? Because I see a lot of buzzwords about authentic coastal experiences, curated local culture, and Instagram-worthy moments. What I don't see is anything about the actual people in this town, the ones who've been running this festival for years."

"The timeline includes multiple community engagement touchpoints—"

"Touchpoints." Bryan shook his head. "You want to turn this into a photo op. Get some influencers to show up and post pretty pictures so tourists will come, spend money, and then leave. That's not what this festival is about."

She gripped the edge of the table. "What it's about is survival. Your attendance is down by nearly forty percent. If you don't make changes, there won't be a festival in five years."

"Maybe that would be better than turning it into a carnival."

"I'm not suggesting a carnival. I'm suggesting professional marketing practices that have been proven to work."

"For corporations. For people who don't care about anything except the bottom line." Bryan stood. "My grandfather started this festival because he wanted to celebrate the community that kept the lighthouse running for generations. It was never supposed to be some branded event designed to extract money from tourists."

"No one is extracting anything." She could hear her voice getting sharper, and she tried to moderate her tone. "I'm trying to help you reach people who would genuinely appreciate what Starlight Shores has to offer. That's not exploitation. That's connection."

"You don't know the first thing about this town. You've been here, what, a week or so? And you think you can waltz in with your fancy presentations and tell us how to do everything better?"

"That's not what I'm doing."

"Then what would you call it?" He gestured at the projector screen. "Because from where I'm sitting, it looks like you're trying to fix something you don't understand."

Mayor West cleared her throat. "Bryan, I think if we just—"

"You want to talk about understanding?" Cassidy cut her off. Her hands were shaking. She pressed them flat against the table. "Let me tell you what I understand. I understand that half the storefronts at the far end of downtown are empty. I understand that your restaurant is struggling to stay afloat. I understand that if this festival fails, you lose one of the few things that still brings people to this town."

Bryan's eyes flashed. "You don't know anything about my restaurant."

"I know you're working eighteen-hour days and still barely breaking even. I know you can't afford to hire enough staff. I know you're one bad season away from losing everything your family built." The words came out cold and hard. "So maybe instead of fighting every suggestion I make, you could consider the possibility that I actually know what I'm talking about."

The room fell silent. Sally set down her bear claw. Marty studied his hands.

Bryan stared at her. Anger flickered across his face, and she swore she also saw hurt, but he quickly covered it.

"You think you've got it all figured out." His voice was quiet now. Dangerous. "You come in here with your statistics and your target demographics and your five-thousand-dollar ad campaigns. You think that's what's going to save us?"

"I think it's a start."

"It's a bandage. You're not solving the actual problems. You're just putting a pretty face on them and hoping tourists won't notice what's underneath." He grabbed his handout and portfolio. "You want to run this your way? Go ahead. I'm sure the mayor would be thrilled to hand it all over to someone with your credentials."

"Bryan—" Mayor West started.

"I'm done." He headed for the door.

Cassidy's pulse pounded in her temples. "We're supposed to be doing this together."

Bryan turned back. "Are we? Because I don't remember being asked if I wanted a co-chair."

The words hit like a slap. Cassidy looked at Mayor West. The mayor's face had gone pink.

"Aren't we at least going to discuss it?" Cassidy forced herself to keep her voice level. "I thought we were co-chairs."

"Whatever would make you think that?" Bryan's eyes stayed on the mayor.

Mayor West shifted in her seat. "Well, you need help, Bryan. You're so busy. And Cassidy has time to help us. It seemed foolish to throw that away."

"Right. Because I can't handle it on my own." Bryan's laugh was bitter. "Fine. You want her? You got her. It's all hers."

He pushed through the door. It swung shut behind him with a bang that rattled the windows.

Nobody spoke. Cassidy stood frozen at the front of the room. Her carefully prepared presentation glowed on the screen behind her. Thirty slides of data and strategy that suddenly felt completely useless.

Mayor West rubbed her temples. "I'll talk to him. He'll come around."

Cassidy sat down. "I don't think he will."

"He's just protective of the festival. It means a lot to him."

"I understand that. I'm not trying to destroy what he's built."

Sally reached over and patted her arm. "We know that, dear."

Did they? Cassidy looked at her presentation materials scattered across the table. Maybe Bryan was right. Maybe she didn't understand anything about this town or what the festival actually meant to the people who lived here.

She'd approached it exactly the way she approached everything. Analyze the problem, identify the solution, and implement the strategy. It was professional and efficient.

But watching Bryan walk out, she'd seen something in his face that her data hadn't captured. The festival wasn't a failing brand that needed repositioning. It was connected to something deeper. His grandfather. His family. The lighthouse itself.

And she'd stood there with her graphs and told him his way wasn't good enough.

Mayor West gathered her things. "Let's reconvene early next week. That'll give everyone time to cool down and think things through."

The others filed out. Cassidy stayed in her seat. She stared at her laptop screen until it dimmed into sleep mode. Her reflection appeared in the black glass. She looked tired.

You don't know the first thing about this town.

He was right. She'd spent days analyzing Starlight Shores like it was a marketing case study, studying demographics, conversion rates, and audience personas. She'd walked past real people having real conversations and saw them only as data points.

The realization settled hard on her. This was exactly what had gotten her here in the first place. Treating everything like a problem to solve, a metric to optimize, and a presentation to deliver. Never stopping to ask if the solution actually served anyone besides her own need to be right.

She closed her laptop. The conference room felt too small suddenly, the air too thick. She needed to get out.

Outside, the morning had heated into a sweltering midday. Tourists wandered past with ice cream cones and shopping bags. A couple took selfies in front of a mural. None of them had any idea that this town was struggling. That's what Bryan had meant about the bandage.

She walked without direction. Her feet carried her toward the waterfront. She ended up at the public dock where fishing boats bobbed in their slips. An older man sat at the end with a rod and a bucket.

"Any luck?" she asked.

He glanced up. "Not yet. Fish are smarter than I am."

She almost smiled. "Mind if I sit?"

"Free country."

She settled onto the weathered wood. Her silk

blouse was definitely ruined. She didn't care. They sat in silence for a while. Gulls circled overhead. The water lapped against the pilings.

"I'm Captain Roy," he said eventually. "And you're the one helping with the festival."

"I was. I'm not sure anymore."

"Heard there was some excitement at the meeting."

Of course he had. She'd forgotten how fast news traveled in small towns. "I made a mess of things."

"Bryan's got a hard head. He comes by it honestly, though. His granddad was the same way."

She watched a pelican dive for fish. It came up empty. "I didn't mean to upset him."

"Probably not. But you did anyway." Captain Roy reeled in his line and checked the bait. "Bryan's been carrying the weight of that festival since his daddy passed away. He took it on himself to keep it going exactly the way it always was. Like if he changed anything, he'd be disrespecting all the people who came before."

"That's not sustainable."

"No. But try telling him that." The old man cast his line back out. "He's scared. That's what it comes down to. Scared he's going to be the one who fails. Scared that if he changes things, they'll slip away anyway, and it'll be his fault for not holding on tight enough."

The words echoed what Winnie had said. She watched the fishing line drift on the current. "How do you help someone who doesn't want to be helped?"

"You stop trying to help and start trying to understand." Captain Roy squinted at her. "That boy doesn't need someone to swoop in and fix everything. He needs someone to stand beside him and admit they're scared too."

She thought about her presentation and all those slides full of solutions. Had she asked Bryan a single question about what he actually wanted? What he feared?

No. She'd told him what to do.

"I need to apologize," she said quietly.

"Probably wouldn't hurt." Captain Roy's rod jerked. He set the hook and started reeling. "Get me that bucket, would you?"

She grabbed the bucket and watched him land a fish. It was a sheepshead, according to Captain Roy. He unhooked it carefully and lowered it back into the water.

"Too small," he explained. "Got to let them grow."

She nodded.

"Thanks for the company," Captain Roy said. "And don't be too hard on yourself. Growing pains hurt. That's how you know it's working."

Cassidy walked back toward the lighthouse. Her mind was already working through what she needed to say to Bryan. Not a pitch. Not a presentation. Just the truth. She was scared too.

CHAPTER 8

Winnie set the delicate teacup on its saucer and watched Sally arrange the scones on a porcelain plate. The lighthouse keeper's quarters always felt smaller when Sally visited. Not in a bad way, but more like the walls leaned in to listen.

"Picked the scones up from the bakery." Sally settled into the chair across from her and reached for her own tea. "I figured I could fill you in on the festival committee meeting disaster."

Winnie raised an eyebrow. "A disaster?"

"Bryan stormed out of that meeting like a hurricane with a personal grudge." Sally broke off a piece of scone and popped it in her mouth. "Linda called me last night. Said she's never seen him that angry."

The tea was too hot. She set it down and let it cool. Outside the window, the Gulf stretched toward the horizon in shades of gray and blue. A seagull swooped past.

She turned back to Sally. "Tell me what happened."

Sally leaned forward. Her eyes had that gleam they always got when she had a good story to tell. "Well, I'm not officially on the committee, but you know how I sit in sometimes to offer help. So, Cassidy showed up with this whole presentation. Slides and everything. Very professional. Very corporate."

"That sounds like Cassidy."

"Well, Bryan didn't take it well." Sally reached for another scone. "He accused her of trying to turn the festival into some kind of theme park attraction. Said she didn't understand the town or what the festival meant to people who'd been here their whole lives."

Winnie sighed. She'd worried something like this might happen.

"Then Cassidy fired back," Sally continued. "Told him his restaurant was struggling and the town's economy was dying. Said they needed fresh ideas, whether he liked it or not."

"Oh dear."

"It got worse." Sally's voice dropped like she was sharing classified information. "Bryan said he never agreed to having a co-chair. That Linda had gone behind his back and undermined him in front of the whole committee."

Winnie picked up her tea again. It had cooled enough to drink. "Linda meant well."

"Of course she did. But you know Bryan. That boy's been shouldering the expectations of three generations since his daddy passed." Sally shook her head. "He's terrified of being the one who fails. And now here comes this fancy executive from the city telling him everything he's done is wrong."

"Is that what Cassidy said?"

"Not in those words. But that's what Bryan heard."

Winnie turned the teacup in her hands. The porcelain was thin and delicate. It had belonged to her grandmother. Generations of Lockhart women had drunk from these cups. She understood about legacy and the fear of failing it.

"You're worried about them," Sally said. It wasn't a question.

"They're both hurting. Bryan's drowning in responsibility he never asked for, and Cassidy's running from something she won't name."

Sally nodded. "I saw her the other day at the store. She was dressed like she was going to a board meeting. In Starlight Shores. On a weekday."

"She doesn't know how to stop moving. Doesn't know who she is if she's not working."

"Sounds lonely."

"I'm sure it is."

They sat in comfortable silence. This was what sixty years of friendship looked like. No need to fill every moment with words.

"You think they can work it out?" Sally asked finally.

"Bryan needs to learn that asking for help doesn't mean admitting defeat, and Cassidy needs to learn that community isn't something you manage. It's something you belong to."

"That's a tall order for both of them."

"Yes."

Sally reached across the table and squeezed Winnie's hand. Her fingers were warm and slightly sticky from the scones. "You'll help them figure it out. You always do."

"I'm not sure they'll listen to an old woman's advice."

"Old woman." Sally snorted. "You've got more sense in your little finger than most people have in their whole body. And they know it. Why do you think everyone ends up on your porch eventually?"

She smiled. "Because I make good tea?"

"Because you see people." Sally leaned back in her chair. "You see what they need before they know they need it. Always have."

The compliment sat awkwardly in the room. She'd never been comfortable with praise. Easier to deflect and move on.

"Another scone?" she offered.

Sally laughed. "Nice try. But I'm serious, Win. Those two are lucky you're watching out for them."

"I'm just a landlord."

"You're family to half this town. Don't pretend you're not."

She looked down at her tea. The surface rippled slightly. Her hand wasn't as steady as it used to be. Getting old was a series of small betrayals. The body giving out in increments. Yet, some days she looked in the mirror, surprised the forty-year-old Winnie wasn't looking back at her.

"Linda told me something else," Sally said. Her voice had shifted, more careful now. "George Morton was in town again yesterday. He was asking questions about the festival. Wanted to know what the attendance numbers were like."

Winnie's spine straightened. "Really? Poking around town?"

"He seemed very interested in whether the festival was financially viable." Sally's eyes narrowed. "You know what that means."

"It means Oceanside Development is still circling."

"Like sharks."

She set her teacup down. The china clinked against the saucer. "They've been after this property for years. The answer is still no."

"I know that. You know that. But if they can

prove the festival isn't sustainable, they'll use it as evidence that the whole waterfront needs to be redeveloped." Sally's mouth pressed into a thin line. "They'll go after Bryan's dock, then the other fishing families. Before you know it, Starlight Shores will be nothing but resort hotels and yacht clubs."

"Not while I'm still breathing."

"That's my girl." Sally grinned. "But it means Cassidy and Bryan need to make this festival work, for more reasons than they realize."

She nodded slowly. The stakes were higher than a simple community celebration. This was about survival and keeping Starlight Shores authentic in the face of developers who saw only profit margins and property values.

"Does Bryan know?" Winnie asked.

"About Morton? Probably. Word has it Morton has already talked to Bryan. But he's got so much on his plate already." Sally sighed. "That boy needs to let someone help carry the load, even if it's someone he doesn't like very much."

"Surely he doesn't dislike Cassidy."

"Could've fooled me after yesterday's fireworks."

"He's afraid of her," Winnie said. "She represents everything he thinks he's failed at."

Sally considered this. "And what's she afraid of?"

"Herself. What she might become if she stops running." Winnie reached for another scone. "She's afraid that if she slows down long enough to feel, she'll realize how empty she is."

Sally shook her head. "You really think they can find their way through all that?"

"I think they don't have a choice. The current's already pulling them together. They can fight it, or they can learn to swim."

"Poetic."

"I'm old. I'm allowed to be poetic."

Sally laughed. It was a good sound, rich and full of life. They'd laughed together through decades of joy and sorrow.

"Thank you for the scones," she said. "And for the company."

"Anytime. You know that." Sally stood and gathered her things. "You going to talk to them? Bryan and Cassidy?"

"If they'll listen."

"They will. Eventually." Sally paused at the door. "You've got a gift for seeing what people need, Win, but don't forget to look at what you need too."

The words hung in the air after Sally left. Winnie sat alone in the keeper's quarters with the remnants of their tea. The house settled around her. The old wood creaked and pipes hummed. The lighthouse had its own language if you knew how to listen.

What did she need?

She carried the dishes to the sink and looked out

at the Gulf. The water moved in eternal rhythms. Tide in. Tide out. Some patterns never changed.

She thought about a boy, so many years ago. About promises made and broken. About the life she'd chosen and the one she'd let slip away.

But she had no use for regrets. They didn't change anything, and they didn't get the dishes washed. She reached for a dishcloth.

CHAPTER 9

The rain started before Cassidy reached the waterfront, not the gentle mist that had rolled in during breakfast, but fat drops that slapped against the pavement and left dark circles on her linen blazer. She should have grabbed an umbrella. She should have changed into something practical. She should have stayed at the cottage and sent an email instead.

But emails were easy. Emails let you hide.

She picked up her pace as the rain intensified. The harbor stretched before her, gray water churning under an equally gray sky. Fishing boats rocked at their moorings, and the wooden planks of the pier gleamed with moisture. Somewhere out there was Bryan Lucas, probably already convinced she was the worst thing to happen to this town since the last hurricane.

He might be right.

She pulled her blazer tighter and stepped onto the pier. The wood creaked under her heels. Water sloshed between the planks, and she could smell the brine and diesel that seemed to define this place. A gull screamed overhead, circling once before disappearing into the storm clouds.

The pier was mostly empty. A few boats bobbed at the far end, and she spotted movement near one of them. A tall figure bent over something on the deck. Even from this distance, she recognized the set of his shoulders.

Of course, he was working in the rain.

She made it halfway down the pier before the wind picked up. It hit her like a physical force and nearly knocked her sideways. She grabbed the railing with one hand and fought to keep her balance. The rain came harder now, driving into her face and soaking through her blazer in seconds.

This was a terrible idea.

But she'd already walked this far, and turning back now would only confirm what Bryan already thought of her. That she was all talk and expensive clothes, someone who gave up the moment things got uncomfortable.

The wind gusted again, and this time she heard something else. A sharp crack, followed by the sound of canvas snapping.

She looked up just in time to see the tent.

It was a large canvas structure filled with crates, and it appeared that someone had forgotten to secure it properly. Now the wind was tearing it loose. The heavy canvas billowed like a sail, straining against the few remaining tie-downs. Metal poles screeched as they bent, and the entire structure lurched toward the edge of the pier, toward the water.

She ran.

Her heels slipped on the wet planks, but she didn't slow down. The tent was massive, easily twenty feet across. If it went into the harbor, it would sink straight to the bottom, along with whatever supplies were stored inside.

She reached the tent just as another gust hit. The canvas ballooned outward, and she grabbed the nearest rope with both hands. The rope burned against her palms as it tried to slip through her grip. She dug her heels in and pulled, but she might as well have been trying to hold back the ocean itself.

The tent lurched forward another foot.

"Hold on!"

Bryan's voice cut through the wind. She didn't turn to look, couldn't spare the attention, but she heard him running across the pier. Then he was there beside her, his hands closing over the rope above hers.

"Pull!" he shouted.

She was already pulling. Her arms screamed with the effort, and her feet slid forward on the slick planks despite her best efforts. The wind howled, and the canvas cracked like a whip.

"The corner!" Bryan jerked his head toward the far side of the tent. "We need to get that pole secured first!"

She looked where he indicated and saw the problem immediately. One of the support poles had come completely loose and was swinging wildly in the wind. If they didn't get it anchored, the whole structure would collapse.

"I'll hold this!" He wrapped the rope around his forearm twice. "Go!"

She didn't argue, didn't point out that she was wearing a linen blazer and heels, or that she'd never secured a tent pole in her life. She just ran.

The pole was heavier than it looked. She grabbed it with both hands. It took everything she had just to keep the pole from swinging into the railing. The wind pushed against her, rain streamed down her face, and her arms felt like they might pull out of their sockets.

She spotted the anchor point, a metal ring bolted to the pier, about six feet away. It might as well have been six miles.

She dragged the pole forward one step at a time. Her heels caught on the planks, and she kicked them off without thinking. The wet wood was rough under her bare feet, but at least she could get traction now. She hauled the pole closer to the ring, muscles burning, lungs screaming.

Almost there.

A gust hit the canvas, and the force traveled down the pole like electricity. Her grip slipped. The pole swung wide, and she lunged after it, catching it just before it could crash into the railing. Her shoulder slammed into the wood, and pain shot down her arm.

"Cassidy!" Bryan's voice was tight with strain. He was still holding the main rope, but she could see him starting to slide forward.

She gritted her teeth and pulled. One more step, then another. Her hands were slippery with rain and probably bleeding, but she didn't let go, couldn't let go.

The ring was right there.

She dropped to her knees and jammed the pole's anchor clip toward the ring. It missed. She tried again, hands shaking, vision blurred by rain and effort. The clip caught the edge of the ring, slipped off, and caught again.

Click.

The pole locked into place, and the tension on that side of the tent immediately eased. She sagged against the railing, gasping for breath.

"The other side!" Bryan was already moving,

rope still wrapped around his arm. "We need to get the other corner down!"

She wanted to tell him she needed a minute, that her arms felt like jelly, and her shoulder throbbed where she'd hit the railing. She wasn't built for this kind of work, had never been built for it, and had spent her entire adult life in climate-controlled offices precisely to avoid moments like this.

Instead, she pushed herself to her feet and ran after him.

The second pole was even worse than the first. It had pulled completely free from its mooring and was dragging along the pier, gouging splinters from the wood. Bryan grabbed it first, and Cassidy threw herself at it a second later. Together, they wrestled it toward the nearest anchor point.

"On three!" Bryan shouted. "One, two—"

They heaved. The pole moved maybe six inches.

"Again!" Bryan's face was set with determination, and rain streamed down his cheeks. "One, two, three!"

This time it moved a foot. Then another. Her feet slipped, and she went down hard on one knee. Pain exploded up her leg, but she didn't let go of the pole. Bryan braced himself against the railing and pulled, and slowly, inch by painful inch, they dragged the pole toward its anchor point.

The wind screamed. The canvas snapped. Her

arms shook with exhaustion, and somewhere in the back of her mind, she registered that her expensive blazer was probably ruined, that her knee was bleeding, and she'd lost both her shoes and would have to walk back to the cottage barefoot.

None of it mattered.

The anchor point was three feet away, then two. Then Bryan was dropping down beside her, hands working to line up the clip with the ring. The pole bucked in their grip, fighting them, but they held on.

The clip caught.

Bryan twisted it into place and locked it down. The tension released all at once, and the tent settled with a final flutter of canvas. The poles held. The ropes held. Everything held.

She collapsed back against the railing. Her chest heaved as she tried to catch her breath. Rain poured down, plastering her hair to her face and turning her once-crisp blazer into a sodden mess. She was covered in grime, splinters, and probably her own blood, and she'd never been so exhausted in her entire life.

Next to her, Bryan sat with his head tipped back against the railing, eyes closed. His shirt was torn at one shoulder, and there was a scrape along his jaw she didn't remember seeing before. He was breathing as hard as she was.

For a long moment, neither of them spoke. The

rain continued to fall, and the wind continued to blow, but the tent stayed secured. They'd done it.

"You okay?" His voice was rough.

She looked down at her hands. They were scraped raw, with rope burns across both palms. Her knee throbbed where she'd hit the pier, and her shoulder wasn't much better. She was soaked to the skin, barefoot, and probably looked like she'd been through a hurricane.

"I'm fine." She started to laugh. She couldn't help it. The absurdity of the situation hit her all at once, and laughter bubbled up despite the exhaustion. "I'm completely fine."

He opened one eye to look at her. Then he started laughing too. Deep, genuine laughter that shook his shoulders and made him wince from the effort.

They sat there in the rain, laughing like idiots while the storm raged around them.

Finally, he pushed himself to his feet. He offered her a hand, and she took it without thinking. His grip was solid and warm, and he pulled her up with an ease that reminded her exactly how strong he was.

"Come on." He gestured toward one of the boats at the end of the pier. "Let's get out of this rain before we drown."

Mary Catherine was larger than she'd expected, a working fishing vessel with a covered deck area and what looked like a small cabin below. Bryan jumped aboard first, then turned to help her across the gap between the pier and the boat. His hand was steady on her arm as she stepped down onto the deck.

The covered area provided immediate relief from the rain. She could still hear it drumming on the roof above them, but at least it wasn't pouring directly onto her head anymore. She wrapped her arms around herself and tried not to shiver.

Bryan disappeared into the cabin and emerged a moment later with two towels and a flannel blanket. He handed her the blanket without a word, and she took it gratefully. The fabric was worn soft from years of use, and it smelled faintly of diesel and salt air.

She wrapped it around her shoulders and finally looked at him properly. Really looked at him.

He looked as exhausted as she felt. The scrape on his jaw was bleeding slightly, and there were rope burns on his hands that matched her own. His shirt was ruined, torn and soaked through, but he'd already grabbed one of the towels and was using it to wipe the rain from his face.

"Thank you," she said quietly. "I wouldn't have been able to hold that on my own."

He lowered the towel and met her eyes. Something had shifted in his expression. The hostility from their previous encounters was gone, replaced by a hint of respect.

"You did good." He nodded toward the tent, now safely secured on the pier. "Most people would have run the other way."

"I thought about it."

"But you didn't." He leaned against the wall of the cabin and crossed his arms. "That's what matters."

The silence that followed wasn't uncomfortable. It was the silence of two people who'd just survived something together, who'd fought side by side against a common enemy and come out the other side still standing.

She pulled the blanket tighter and tried to ignore the way her hands were starting to shake now that the adrenaline was wearing off. She'd done physical work before, of course. Gym sessions, yoga classes, and the occasional corporate team-building exercise that involved climbing walls or navigating obstacle courses. But this had been different. This had been real.

"I came to apologize," she said finally. "For the meeting. For steamrolling over your concerns and acting like I knew better than everyone who's actually lived here."

He raised an eyebrow. "That's why you were looking for me?"

"Yes." She met his gaze directly. "I was wrong about a lot of things. I treated the festival like a marketing case study instead of something that actually matters to people. To you."

He studied her for a long moment, and she fought the urge to fill the silence with more words and defend herself the way she always did. Instead, she waited.

"I wasn't exactly welcoming either," he admitted. "I saw you walk into that meeting with your fancy clothes and your marketing degree, and I assumed you were just another outsider trying to fix something that wasn't broken."

"It is a little broken, though," she said carefully. "The festival, I mean. The attendance numbers, the budget issues, and the fact that half the town seems to think it's not worth the effort anymore."

"I know." He scrubbed a hand over his face. "I've known for a while. I just didn't want to admit it because that would mean admitting that maybe I'm not doing a good enough job and that maybe I'm the one who's letting everyone down."

The vulnerability in his voice caught her off guard. This was the man who'd stood up in that committee meeting and accused her of trying to destroy everything his family had built. But underneath the anger and the defensiveness, he was just scared of failing.

She understood that fear better than she wanted to admit.

"You're not letting anyone down. You're trying

to hold together an entire town's tradition while running a restaurant and a fishing business and probably a dozen other things I don't even know about. That's not failure. That's just impossible."

He shrugged. "My grandfather did it. My father did it."

"Did they do it alone?"

The question hung in the air between them. Bryan looked away, staring out at the rain-soaked harbor. The storm was starting to ease, the wind dropping from a howl to a steady push. The worst of it was over.

"No," he said finally. "They had help. The whole town helped back then. But things are different now. People are stretched thin. Everyone's fighting their own battles."

"Then maybe we need to stop fighting and start working together." She adjusted the blanket around her shoulders. "I know you don't trust me yet. I get that. But I'm not here to turn your festival into some corporate event. I just want to help make it successful. The way it used to be."

He turned back to face her. His expression was still guarded but hopeful. "You really mean that?"

"I do." She held out her scraped, rope-burned hand. "Truce?"

He looked at her hand for a moment, then at her face. Whatever he saw there must have satisfied him because he reached out and clasped her hand firmly. His grip was warm and rough, and she felt something shift inside her. Not attraction exactly, though she couldn't deny he was handsome in a rugged, practical way that was completely different from the polished corporate men she usually dated.

"Truce," he agreed. "But I have conditions."

"Of course you do." She hid a smile. "Let's hear them."

"First, you actually listen when people tell you why something matters to them. Not just nod and then do what you were planning to do anyway."

"Fair."

"Second, any changes we make have to honor what the festival's always been about. This isn't just a tourist event. It's how this town celebrates itself."

"Agreed." She nodded. "What else?"

"Third, you stop wearing heels to the waterfront. You're going to break your neck."

She laughed, surprised by the concern hidden in his gruff tone. "I'll add it to my list of new rules for small-town living."

"There are a lot of those." He released her hand and leaned back against the cabin wall. "You're going to need a longer list."

The rain had slowed to a drizzle. Through the gap in the clouds, she could see a strip of lighter sky on the horizon. The storm was passing, leaving behind wet wood and clean air.

She looked down at her ruined blazer, her bare

feet, and her scraped hands. A few weeks ago, she would have been horrified by her appearance and would have rushed back to her car and driven straight to the nearest hotel to clean up and restore order. Now she just felt tired and oddly satisfied.

"I should get back," she said reluctantly.

"I'll walk you." He pushed away from the wall. "The pier's slippery after a storm."

"I'm barefoot. I think slippery is the least of my problems."

"All the more reason." He grabbed another towel from the cabin and handed it to her. "At least dry off a little more first."

She took the towel and did her best to squeeze some of the water from her hair. It was a lost cause, but the effort made her feel slightly more human. When she looked up, Bryan was watching her with an expression she couldn't quite read.

"What?"

"Nothing." He shook his head. "Just trying to figure you out."

"Good luck with that." She wrapped the towel around her shoulders, layering it over the blanket. "I've been trying to figure myself out for a lot of years, and I'm still working on it."

They made their way back across the pier together. Bryan's hand hovered near her elbow, not quite touching but ready to steady her if she slipped.

It was an old-fashioned gesture, protective without being patronizing, and she found she didn't mind it.

The storm had left everything washed clean and gleaming. The boats rocked gently at their moorings, and the smell of rain mixed with salt air created something fresh and new. She breathed it in and felt some of the tension she'd been carrying for weeks finally start to ease.

Maybe this sabbatical wasn't career suicide after all. Maybe it was something else entirely.

"Same time tomorrow?" he asked when they reached the end of the pier. "For the committee meeting?"

"I'll be there." She glanced back at the secured tent. "And I'll bring better ideas this time. Ones that actually take your concerns into account."

"I'll try to be less of a jerk about shooting them down."

"Deal."

They stood there for another moment, neither quite ready to walk away. The easy hostility that had defined their previous interactions was gone, replaced by something more complicated. Partnership, maybe. Or at least the potential for it.

Finally, he cleared his throat. "You need a ride back to the lighthouse? You can't walk all that way barefoot."

She looked down at her feet, then at the long

stretch of road leading back to Heron Cottage. He had a point.

"That would be great, actually. Thank you."

As they walked toward Bryan's truck, she caught sight of her reflection in a shop window. She looked like she'd been through a hurricane—soaked, disheveled, covered in grime. Her carefully maintained professional image had been completely destroyed.

And somehow, she didn't mind.

CHAPTER 10

Cassidy woke to the sound of rain drumming against the cottage windows and every muscle in her body staging a protest. Her shoulders ached. Her palms burned. Even her calves complained about yesterday's sprint across the dock in three-inch heels.

She sat up slowly and winced. The bedside clock read 6:47 AM, which meant she'd actually slept past her usual 5:30 alarm. When was the last time that happened?

Her phone sat on the nightstand, mercifully silent. No urgent emails from the office. No passive-aggressive messages from Steve about campaign strategies he was implementing in her absence. Just a weather alert about continued storms through the afternoon and a text from Mayor West thanking her for "heroic tent rescue efforts."

Cassidy set the phone down and examined her hands. Raw rope burns crossed both palms, the skin angry and red. She'd refused Bryan's offer of first aid supplies last night, too exhausted and rain-soaked to do anything but accept the ride home and collapse into bed fully dressed.

Well, almost fully dressed. She'd managed to peel off her ruined blazer before falling face-first into the pillow.

She stood and caught her reflection in the mirror. Her hair stuck up at odd angles. Yesterday's mascara had migrated south. The white blouse she'd chosen so carefully was wrinkled beyond salvation and spotted with what looked like rust stains from the tent poles.

She looked absolutely terrible.

The thought made her smile.

She grabbed her robe and padded to the kitchen. There was a note taped to the window: *Open the door.*

She opened the door and discovered Winnie had left a covered plate of blueberry muffins on the table. A note in elegant handwriting read: *Heard you had quite an adventure. These help with everything. —W.*

The muffins were still slightly warm. She broke one open and took a bite, then carried the plate to the sunroom. The windows were all soft morning light despite the gray skies.

She settled into the cushioned chair and looked

out at the rain-swept courtyard.Winnie's garden bent under the wind but didn't break. Everything looked wild and alive, completely indifferent to schedules or productivity metrics.

She ate another muffin and tried to remember the last time she'd sat still without her laptop open. The last time she'd looked at something just to look at it, not to analyze or optimize or extract value from the experience.

Her mind kept circling back to yesterday. To Bryan's face when she'd grabbed those ropes. The way he'd run toward the danger instead of away from it, no hesitation, just immediate action. How they'd worked together without discussion, each anticipating the other's movements.

Her phone buzzed. She almost ignored it, then glanced at the screen.

Bryan: *Checking if you survived the night. Also checking if you need medical attention for those hands.*

She looked at her palms again. They really did hurt.

She typed: *Survived. Hands are fine. How's the tent?*

The reply came quickly: *Dry. Unlike everything else in this town. Committee meeting's postponed because of the weather. Thought you should know.*

She answered: *Thanks for the update.*

Three dots appeared, then disappeared, then appeared again. Finally: *The apology yesterday. I should've said this then, but I was too wet and tired. I appreciate it. Takes guts to admit when you're wrong.*

She stared at the message. In her corporate world, apologies were strategic maneuvers, carefully worded non-apologies designed to deflect blame while appearing conciliatory.

She typed: *Takes guts to accept help when you don't want to need it.*

She could almost hear his laugh: *Yeah. Working on that.*

She smiled as she replied: *Me too.*

The conversation ended there, but she kept looking at the screen. Something had shifted yesterday on that dock. Some wall she'd built between herself and everything that wasn't work had developed a crack.

She set the phone aside and pulled her laptop onto her lap. Muscle memory. It felt comforting and familiar. She opened the screen and stared at her desktop, organized into color-coded folders with labels like "Q3 Strategy" and "Phillips Pitch Materials."

Her cursor hovered over her email.

Just to check. Just to see if anything urgent came through overnight.

She closed the laptop.

The rain continued its steady drumming against the windows. She sat in the sunroom, hands aching, body sore, doing absolutely nothing productive.

It felt strange. Uncomfortable. Like wearing shoes that didn't quite fit.

But it didn't feel wrong.

By afternoon, the storm had settled into a steady drizzle. She showered, applied antiseptic cream to her palms, and dressed in jeans and a soft sweater. The casual clothes felt foreign after trying to maintain her professional armor, but it was time for a change.

She was contemplating lunch when someone knocked on the cottage door.

Bryan stood on her porch holding a white paper bag and two disposable coffee cups. Water dripped from his jacket. His hair was plastered to his forehead.

"I brought food," he said. "And coffee. Figured you might not want to venture out in this mess."

She stepped back to let him in. "You didn't have to do that."

"I know." He handed her one of the cups and set the bag on her kitchen counter. "But I wanted to talk about the festival without an audience. Thought this might be easier than meeting at Harbor Brew with half the town watching."

"Good point." She opened the bag and found two wrapped sandwiches from the Sandpiper. The smell made her stomach growl. "I haven't eaten since the muffins this morning."

"Winnie's blueberry ones?"

"How did you know?"

"She has a sixth sense about when people need baked goods." He pulled out one of the kitchen chairs and sat. "I've lived here my whole life, and I still don't know how she does it."

She unwrapped her sandwich and took a bite. Fresh grouper, perfectly seasoned, with some kind of citrus aioli that made her want to ask for the recipe. "This is incredible."

"Family recipe. My grandmother's. She used to make these for festival volunteers. Said good food was the foundation of community."

"She sounds wise."

"She was." He picked at his own sandwich. "She's the one who taught me that the festival wasn't about the events or the attendance numbers. It was about giving people a reason to gather. To remember they belonged to something bigger than themselves."

She set down her sandwich. "I didn't understand that before. I was treating it like a marketing campaign. Build awareness, drive attendance, measure ROI."

"That's what you know how to do."

"But it's not what the festival needs." She wrapped her hands around her coffee cup, feeling the warmth through her bandaged palms. "I've been thinking about what you said about the festival being tied to your memories of your grandfather."

He looked up. "Yeah?"

"My mother used to drag me to this street fair every summer when I was a kid. Small-town thing, nothing fancy. Local bands, craft booths, and funnel cakes." She heard herself talking and couldn't quite believe it. She never shared personal stories. "I hated it. Thought it was boring and unsophisticated. I wanted to be anywhere else. But now..."

"Now?"

"Now, even though I don't like to admit it, I think back about it and I... miss it."

"You should go back to one again."

"Well, Mom would love that, but it seems like I'm always too busy."

"We make time for what's important."

She nodded. "You're right. I just didn't want to... to get trapped back in that small-town life."

A hint of hurt flashed across his eyes, but he quickly recovered. "So you're a confirmed city girl."

"Guess so." She shrugged. "I've spent years building a career in the city, and I'm good at what I do. But I don't belong to anything. I don't have a community. I just have a network of professional contacts and an apartment I sleep in between business trips."

The admission hung in the air between them. She waited for Bryan to offer platitudes or change the subject. Instead, he nodded slowly.

"I've been so afraid of losing what my family built that I couldn't see I was losing it anyway," he said. "The fishing industry's dying. The restaurant's struggling. The festival's attendance drops every year. And I keep trying to hold everything exactly as it was, like if I just work hard enough and refuse to change, I can freeze time."

"That's not how time works."

"No kidding." He frowned. "George Morton, a developer from Oceanside Development, offered to buy the restaurant and our dock rights. Told me the waterfront's getting redeveloped whether I cooperate or not."

"Oceanside Development?" A cold wave of apprehension washed over her.

"Yeah. You know them?"

"I know companies like them. They'll turn this whole waterfront into high-end retail and resort properties. They'll price out all the locals, destroy the working harbor, and replace authenticity with something photogenic and profitable." She thought of her presentation, with its talk of target demographics and visitor experience optimization. "I almost helped them do it."

"What?"

"Not intentionally. But my whole approach was about making Starlight Shores more marketable and more appealing to tourists. I wasn't thinking about what that would cost the people who actually live here." She pushed her sandwich away, appetite gone. "I'm part of the problem."

"No, you were trying to help. You just didn't have all the information."

"I should've asked more questions before proposing solutions."

"Yeah, probably." He grinned. "But I should've been willing to listen instead of assuming you were the enemy."

They sat in comfortable silence while rain continued to fall outside. She finished her coffee and thought about her color-coded schedules and strategic frameworks. All those tools that worked perfectly in her corporate world but meant nothing here.

"I don't know how to do this," she admitted. "How to help without fixing and how to contribute without controlling."

"Welcome to my world." He stood and carried their trash to the trashcan. "I've been trying to figure that out with the festival for the last few years. How to honor tradition while accepting change, and preserve what matters while letting go of what doesn't."

"Any luck?"

"Not yet." He paused at her door. "But maybe we figure it out together. You bring the marketing expertise. I bring the local knowledge. We both bring the willingness to admit when we're wrong."

"Deal." She walked him to the door. "Thank you for the sandwich."

"Thank you for grabbing that tent yesterday. You saved thousands of dollars in supplies. It's kind of our community storage for the fishermen. We should probably find something a bit sturdier."

"You would've done the same."

"Yeah, but I wouldn't have done it in designer heels." His grin was genuine this time. "That was impressive."

After he left, she returned to the sunroom and opened her laptop. But instead of checking email, she created a new document and titled it "Festival Planning Notes."

She started writing questions instead of solutions. What did the festival mean to longtime residents? What traditions mattered most? What changes would honor the past while building toward the future?

Outside, the rain finally stopped.

CHAPTER 11

The next morning, the storm had passed, leaving everything washed clean and bright. Cassidy sat up in bed and stretched carefully, testing her sore muscles. Still tender, but better than yesterday.

She dressed in shorts and a lightweight sweater, then grabbed her laptop bag. The urge to check her work email had faded to a dull background hum instead of the screaming urgency she'd felt a week ago. Progress, maybe. Or just distraction.

Either way, she was heading to Harbor Brew.

To her surprise, she decided to take the long way into town along the waterfront path. It took twenty-five minutes, and she didn't even think about hurrying. The Gulf sparkled under the morning sun, all traces of yesterday's violence erased. Pelicans dove for fish. A couple walked their dog along the waterfront. Everything looked peaceful and timeless, like the storm had never happened.

Harbor Brew was busy. The line stretched to the door, and every table was occupied. Cassidy joined the queue and scanned the room. The four elderly women she'd seen the other day occupied their same corner table, heads bent together in serious conversation. Marty Fuller browsed the community bulletin board, adding a flyer for some upcoming bookstore event.

"Cassidy!" Jan waved from behind the counter. "Your usual?"

She had a usual now. When had that happened?

"Please," she said, then added, "and one of those lemon scones."

"Coming right up." Jan started preparing her coffee. "Heard you saved the day. Whole town's talking about you and Bryan wrestling that tent in the storm."

"News travels fast."

"Honey, this is Starlight Shores. News travels before it happens." Jan set the coffee and scone on the counter. "Those hands healing okay?"

She held up her bandaged palms. "Getting there."

"You need anything, you let me know. We take care of our own around here." Jan turned to the next customer, leaving Cassidy to process that statement.

Our own. Like she belonged here. Like two weeks and one dramatic tent rescue had somehow earned her a place in this community.

She found a small table near the window and settled in with her coffee. The scone was perfect, tart, sweet, and buttery. She broke off a piece and watched the room.

The four elderly women were still deep in conversation. One of them, the sharp-eyed woman, gestured emphatically. The others nodded in agreement.

Jan appeared with a coffee pot, refilling cups at nearby tables. When she reached Cassidy's, she topped it off despite it being nearly full.

"Those ladies over there," Cassidy said, nodding toward the corner table. "They come here often?"

"Three or four times a week. The Harbor Ladies Club." Jan grinned. "At least, that's what they call themselves. Rest of us have other names for them, but those aren't polite enough to repeat before noon."

"They seem very... involved."

"That's one word for it. They know everything that happens in this town before it happens. Got their fingers in every pie, their opinions on every topic, and their judgment on every newcomer." Jan lowered her voice. "But between you and me? They volunteer more hours than anyone else combined. Food drives, beach cleanups, school fundraisers, you name it. They complain the whole time, but they show up."

She looked at the women with newfound appreciation. "Think they'd help with the festival?"

Jan's expression turned doubtful. "Maybe. If you can convince them you're not going to ruin everything they love about it."

"Bryan said the same thing."

"Bryan's not wrong." Jan moved to the next table, leaving her alone with her thoughts.

She ate her scone and tried to strategize. In her corporate world, she'd approach this like any stakeholder management challenge. She'd identify key influencers, understand their concerns, and address objections with data and logic.

But that was exactly the wrong approach here. She'd learned that lesson the hard way at the committee meeting.

She was still debating her next move when Sally Morris walked in. She grabbed coffee, spotted Cassidy, and headed straight for her table.

"Mind if I join you?" Sally asked.

"Please." She gestured to the empty chair.

Sally took a quick sip. "Heard you had quite an adventure the other day."

"The tent rescue?"

"The whole town heard about it. You and Bryan working together, saving thousands of dollars' worth of supplies, getting soaked to the bone in the process." Sally's eyes twinkled. "Romantic, some folks are saying."

Cassidy felt heat creep up her neck. "It wasn't romantic. It was practical. The tent was about to blow into the harbor."

"Mmm-hmm." Sally didn't look convinced. "And how are things going with the festival planning?"

"Honestly? I'm not sure." She wrapped her hands around her coffee cup. "I thought I could help. Bring some professional expertise, modern marketing strategies, and a fresh perspective. But everyone keeps telling me I don't understand what the festival means to this community."

"Do you?"

"Bryan talked about it a bit. I know it means a lot to him. But no, I don't really know what it means to everyone."

Sally nodded approvingly. "That's a good start. Admitting what you don't know."

"But how do I learn? Bryan's willing to work with me now, but everyone else still sees me as an outsider who's going to ruin everything."

Sally's lips curved in a wry smile. "From your previous approach to the festival, they're not completely wrong."

"So what do I do?"

Sally set down her coffee and looked at Cassidy with the kind of direct, assessing gaze that made her feel like a balance sheet being audited. "You ask. You listen. You learn."

"That's it?"

"That's everything." Sally leaned back in her chair. "You want to know what the festival means to this community? Ask people. Not as a marketing consultant doing research, but as a person who genuinely wants to understand."

She thought about her presentation slides and her target demographic analysis. Those tools that created distance between her and the actual human beings she was supposed to be helping.

"What does it mean to you?" she asked.

Sally's expression softened. "The festival's been part of my life forever. Started right before I was born. I've watched children grow up through it. The first time they enter the sandcastle contest, then years later they're volunteering at the information booth, then they're bringing their own kids to enter the sandcastle contest." She smiled at some private memory. "My late husband proposed to me at the festival, during the boat parade, with all those lights reflecting on the water."

"That's beautiful."

"It was perfect." Sally's eyes clouded for a moment. She shook her head and smiled. "The festival isn't about attendance numbers or economic impact. It's about continuity. About gathering together year after year and remembering who we are, where we come from, and what we've built together."

She felt something shift in her understanding. "I've been approaching this all wrong."

"You've been approaching it the way you know how. That's not wrong, it's just incomplete." Sally stood and collected her coffee. "Talk to people, Cassidy. Really talk to them. You might be surprised what you learn."

After Sally left, Cassidy sat with her half-finished coffee and thought about continuity. About gathering year after year and remembering who you are.

She couldn't remember the last time she'd attended the same event two years in a row. Her life was a series of new campaigns, new clients, and new strategies. Always moving forward, never looking back, and measuring success by what she'd achieved lately rather than what she'd built over time.

She looked at the Harbor Ladies Club table again. The four women were still talking, their conversation animated but warm. Whatever they were discussing, they were fully engaged with each other and the topic.

She stood before she could talk herself out of it. She crossed the coffee shop and stopped at their table.

Four pairs of eyes turned to her. The sharp-eyed woman raised an eyebrow.

"I'm sorry to interrupt," Cassidy said. "I'm Cassidy Wren."

"We know." The woman didn't offer her name.

"I'm working with Bryan on the Harbor Festival."

One woman snorted.

Cassidy took a breath. "But I've approached it all wrong, like I would a corporate client. I'm hoping you might help me understand what the festival means to the community. To you all."

The women exchanged glances. Some silent communication passed between them.

"Sit down," the sharp-eyed woman finally said.

Cassidy pulled over a chair from an empty table and sat on the edge, feeling like a job applicant at an interview.

"I'm Dorothy," the sharp-eyed woman said. "This is Margaret, Ruth, and Helen." She pointed to each woman in turn. They nodded but didn't smile.

"Nice to meet you all."

"Jan says you're helping Bryan chair the festival committee," Margaret said. She was the smallest of the four, with white curls and a surprisingly strong voice.

"I'm trying to help. If Bryan will let me. If any of you will let me."

"Why should we?" Ruth asked. She wore a visor

and had the tanned, weathered look of someone who spent serious time outdoors.

It was a fair question. Cassidy had asked herself the same thing a dozen times.

"Because I want to learn," she said honestly. "I came to Starlight Shores on mandatory sabbatical, completely burned out from my corporate job. I thought I'd spend two months sitting on the beach, proving I was fine, then go back to my real life." She looked at her bandaged hands. "But something's changing. This place is changing me. The festival could be just another project, another line on my resume. Or it could be something real. Something that matters."

"Pretty words," Helen said. She was the largest of the four, with steel-gray hair cut short and direct brown eyes. "But we've heard pretty words before. Developers come through here all the time with pretty words about preservation and community character. Then they buy up the waterfront and turn it into resort properties."

"I'm not a developer."

"No, but you're a marketing consultant. Same difference, in my book. You package things up and sell them to the highest bidder."

The accusation stung because it was partially true. How many campaigns had she created that prioritized profit over people? How many times had she optimized away the messy human elements to create a cleaner brand story?

"You're right," she said. "That's what I do in my regular job. That's what I was trying to do with the festival at first. But I don't want to do that anymore."

"Why not?" Dorothy asked.

"Because Sally just told me about her husband proposing during the boat parade. Because Bryan talked about his grandmother teaching him that good food is the foundation of community. Because Winnie leaves muffins outside my door when she knows I need them." She felt unexpected emotion rise in her throat. "Because I've spent years building a career and I have nothing. No community. No traditions. No continuity. Just an apartment I sleep in between business trips and a network of professional contacts who are probably forgetting my name while I'm gone."

The four women were quiet. She'd said too much. Revealed too much. Shown weakness to people who had no reason to trust her.

"The festival started seventy-four years ago," Dorothy said slowly. "My family helped the Lucas family organize the first one. Just a small gathering, really. Some local artists selling their work, a few food vendors, Bryan's grandfather grilling fish on the beach. Maybe two hundred people showed up."

"It grew every year," Margaret added. "More

vendors, more visitors, more events. They added the boat parade after a few years. The sandcastle contest came later. The lighthouse tours came later after Winnie took over being lighthouse keeper."

"My granddaughter won the sandcastle contest when she was eight," Ruth said. "She's twenty-six now, lives in Tampa, but she still comes back every year for the festival. Brings her friends. Says it's her favorite weekend of the year."

"That's what the festival is," Helen finished. "It's seventy-four years of memories. It's sandcastles and fish grilled on the beach. It's watching children grow up and move away, but come back because this is home."

She nodded, not trusting her voice.

"So when you come in with your slides and fancy terms," Dorothy continued, "we see someone who wants to turn all that into data points. Someone who thinks success is measured in attendance numbers instead of connections made."

"I'm beginning to understand," she managed.

"Do you?" Dorothy's sharp eyes studied her. "Because if you really understand, then you know we can't let you destroy what we've built. Even if it means the festival gets smaller. Even if it means we struggle financially."

"I don't want to destroy anything." She met Dorothy's gaze. "I want to learn. I want to help. But I need you to teach me what matters and what doesn't. What can change and what needs to stay the same."

The four women looked at each other again. More silent communication.

"We meet here every Tuesday and Thursday morning," Dorothy finally said. "Nine o'clock. We've been volunteering with the festival forever. We know every vendor, every tradition, every story." She paused. "You can join us if you want. Listen to what we're planning. Ask your questions. Learn what you need to learn."

"Really?"

"But if you try to turn this into some corporate initiative, we'll vote you off the committee so fast your head will spin," Helen added. "We've done it before. We'll do it again."

"Understood." She stood. "Thank you. I'll be here Tuesday morning."

She walked back to her table on shaky legs. She'd just been granted provisional acceptance by the Harbor Ladies Club. It felt more significant than any corporate promotion she'd ever received.

Her phone buzzed with an email notification. She glanced at the screen and saw Steve's name. Something about the Phillips pitch meeting being moved up.

She silenced the phone and slipped it into her bag.

CHAPTER 12

The next morning, Cassidy woke with a sense of purpose she hadn't felt in weeks. She wasn't filled with the caffeine-fueled urgency that had driven her corporate life, but something steadier and more grounded.

She had a project. Not just a marketing campaign or a client deliverable, but something real. Something that mattered to actual people with actual memories and actual lives.

She dressed in shorts—she only had two pairs and should really go shopping—and a cotton shirt, then grabbed her laptop bag. Before leaving, she paused at the sunroom window. The Gulf stretched out calm and blue under the morning sun. A few boats dotted the horizon. Everything looked peaceful.

Her phone sat on the kitchen counter where

she'd left it last night. She picked it up and saw three new emails from work. She set it back down without opening them.

Progress.

She found Winnie in the courtyard garden, deadheading a gardenia bush. The older woman looked up and smiled.

"Morning, dear. You're up early."

"I wanted to ask you something." She set down her bag. "I'm working on understanding the festival better. The Harbor Ladies were helpful when they talked to me yesterday."

"The Harbor Ladies Club talked with you? That's progress."

"A bit. But I want to show them and Bryan that I really am interested in learning what the festival means to the town. I thought it might be useful to look at historical photos. Maybe old newspaper clippings. Get a sense of how it's evolved over the years."

Winnie snipped another dead bloom. "That's a good idea. The lighthouse museum has quite a collection. Festival photos, old editions of The Beacon, various records, and documents. You're welcome to look through anything you'd like."

"Really? I wouldn't be intruding?"

"The museum exists to preserve our history. Can't do that if no one ever looks at it." Winnie straightened and brushed dirt from her hands. "Come on. I'll show you where everything is."

The lighthouse museum occupied a small building off the lightkeeper's cottage. Winnie opened the door and led her into a circular room with whitewashed walls and tall windows.

Display cases lined the perimeter, filled with old navigation equipment, vintage photographs, and logbooks with careful handwritten entries. A model of the lighthouse as it had looked in 1885 occupied a central table.

"The archives are back here." Metal shelving units held labeled boxes and binders. "Festival materials are on the middle shelf. Newspaper archives are over there. Take your time. If you need anything, I'll be in the keeper's quarters."

"Thank you, Winnie."

"My pleasure." Winnie paused at the door. "It's good to see you taking an interest in our history. Understanding where we've been helps us figure out where we're going."

After Winnie left, Cassidy stood in the archive room and felt slightly overwhelmed. There were dozens of boxes, decades of materials. She could spend weeks here.

She started with the festival files. The first box held photos from the inaugural event years ago. An older photo showed a man—she assumed was Bryan's grandfather—at a grill, smoke rising around him as he cooked fish. The crowd was small, maybe two hundred people like Dorothy had said, but everyone looked happy.

The second box held materials from later years. She found the first boat parade photos with strings of lights and lanterns reflecting on dark water. The first sandcastle contest, with children kneeling in the sand while parents watched. A newspaper clipping with the headline "Starlight Harbor Festival Draws Record Crowd" and a photo of a mayor cutting a ribbon.

She pulled out her phone and started taking pictures. These would be perfect for a historical timeline in the festival brochure. Not slick marketing photos, but real moments. Real people. Real community.

The third box held financial records. She almost skipped it, but her corporate training made her curious. She pulled out a ledger from fifteen years ago and flipped through vendor fees, sponsorship contributions, and expense reports.

Everything looked normal. Small-town festival finances, carefully tracked by volunteers who probably had no formal accounting training but knew how to balance a checkbook.

She was about to put it back when she noticed another box on a lower shelf. It was older, the cardboard worn at the edges. The label read "Lighthouse Operations 1940-1950."

That wasn't festival material, but something made her pull it out anyway.

Inside were leather-bound logbooks, their pages yellowed with age. She opened one carefully and found daily entries in neat handwriting. Weather conditions, ship sightings, and maintenance notes. The mundane record of lighthouse operations.

She opened it and turned the pages. At the year 1943, she found an entry that made her pause.

March 15, 1943. Official ceremony held. Lighthouse operations to continue under private arrangement.

She kept reading. The entries continued without interruption. Same handwriting, same level of detail. Daily weather, ship traffic, and routine maintenance. As if nothing had changed.

She pulled out another logbook and found financial records. A separate ledger tracked expenses and income. After March 1943, the entries showed Private Trust Funding as the source for all operational costs. Significant amounts, enough to maintain a full staff and keep the lighthouse running at peak efficiency.

The government funded lighthouses. Who was funding *this* lighthouse?

She dug deeper and found a manila folder of photographs. Most showed the lighthouse from various angles and documentation of structural changes over the years. But one photo made her stop.

It showed the interior of the lighthouse. Five men stood around a table covered with equipment. Not navigation equipment. Radio equipment. Sophisticated-looking devices with dials, switches, and antenna connections.

She turned the photo over. Someone had written on the back in faded ink: *Henry Lockhart and Academic Consultants, 1940.*

Academic consultants? At a lighthouse?

She looked at the photo again. Henry Lockhart stood in the center, a tall man with serious eyes. The other men wore suits and ties, inappropriate for lighthouse work. They looked like professors or researchers, not sailors or engineers.

And that equipment definitely wasn't standard lighthouse gear.

She took several photos with her phone, then carefully replaced everything in the boxes. Her mind raced with questions.

She found Winnie in the keeper's quarters, sitting at her kitchen table with a cup of tea and the newspaper.

"Find what you needed?" Winnie asked.

"Yes. The festival photos are perfect." She set her bag on the table. "But I found something else. Something I don't understand."

Winnie's expression didn't change, but something flickered in her eyes. "What's that?"

She pulled out her phone, scrolled past the

photos of the festival, and showed Winnie the photo of the financial ledger entry. "This says the lighthouse was under private funding in 1943. But the government pays for lighthouse maintenance and use, right? How is that possible?"

"The government stopped funding it. We fought for private ownership instead." Winnie's voice was calm, matter-of-fact. "My grandfather established a trust to cover operational costs."

"That must have been expensive."

"It was important to the family."

She showed Winnie the photo of Henry Lockhart and the academic consultants. "What about this? Who were these men?"

Winnie studied the photo for a long moment. "I don't know. I wasn't born when that was taken. But men in suits came to visit my father sometimes. Important-looking men with briefcases and serious faces."

"Academic consultants?"

"That's what my father called them. He'd tell me to go play with Sally when they arrived. Said they had boring grown-up business to discuss." Winnie smiled slightly. "I thought they were probably university professors. My father was interested in maritime history and lighthouse engineering. I assumed they were colleagues."

"But you don't know for sure?"

"My father didn't discuss those details of his

work with me. I was a child, and then a young woman with other concerns. By the time I was old enough to ask serious questions, he'd had his heart attack and passed away." Winnie set down her teacup. "Whatever secrets he kept are buried with him."

She looked at the photo again. Something about it nagged at her. The equipment, the formal dress, the serious expressions. It didn't look like an academic consultation. It looked like something else.

"What about the private trust? Is it still active?"

"Yes. It provides some funding for lighthouse maintenance. The cottage rentals cover the rest. Usually." Winnie stood and refilled her teacup. "Why all these questions? I thought you were researching the festival."

"I am. I was. But this is interesting."

"History usually is." Winnie returned to her seat. "But some history is just history. Old photos and financial records from years ago. Fascinating for researchers, perhaps, but not particularly relevant to your festival planning."

It was a gentle dismissal, but a dismissal nonetheless.

She nodded slowly. "You're right. I should focus on the festival materials. That's what I came here for."

"Good idea." Winnie smiled warmly. "Those historical photos you found will make a wonderful addition to your brochure. People love seeing how things used to be."

She gathered her bag and thanked Winnie for access to the archives. But as she walked back to Heron Cottage, she couldn't stop thinking about that photo.

Academic consultants. Sophisticated radio equipment. A lighthouse that was officially decommissioned but kept running with mysterious private funding.

Her instincts recognized a story that didn't quite add up. Details that didn't fit the official narrative.

But Winnie had made it clear the subject was closed. Whatever had happened in 1940, whatever those men in suits had been doing, it was none of her business.

She should let it go. Focus on the festival. That's what she was here for.

Back at the cottage, she opened her laptop and started organizing the festival photos chronologically. They really would make a great brochure. She could already see the layout: "Seventy-Four Years of Community" as the headline, with a timeline showing how the event had grown and evolved.

Her phone buzzed. Another work email. She flipped her phone facedown.

CHAPTER 13

Bryan pushed through the door of Harbor Brew, scanning the crowded coffee shop for Cassidy. He spotted her immediately at the corner table, surrounded by the Harbor Ladies Club like some kind of corporate diplomat who'd wandered into enemy territory and somehow survived.

He should probably rescue her. Those four women could reduce grown men to stammering apologies with nothing more than a pointed look and a well-timed sigh.

Except she wasn't stammering. She was laughing.

"Dorothy, I absolutely agree," Cassidy said as she leaned forward with her hands wrapped around a coffee mug. "The traditional fish fry has to be the centerpiece. But what if we also added a recipe contest? Local families could submit their best seafood dishes, and we'd feature the winners at the festival. It honors the cooking traditions while getting more people involved."

Dorothy, the most formidable of the Harbor Ladies, tilted her head with approval. "You're saying people would compete to be part of the menu?"

"Exactly. We could call it the Starlight Shores Heritage Recipe Competition. First place gets their dish featured with their family name on the festival program. It's not about changing tradition. It's about celebrating it."

"Hmm." Dorothy exchanged glances with the other three women. "That might work."

He blinked. Dorothy had just said something might work. To an outsider. To Cassidy Wren, who less than two weeks ago had been public enemy number one for suggesting they needed to change anything at all.

"I'll draft the competition rules this afternoon," Cassidy continued. She pulled out her phone and started typing notes. "We should probably cap entries at twenty to keep judging manageable. And we'll need a panel of judges. Would the four of you be willing to serve?"

Jan appeared at his elbow with a knowing smile. "She's been at it for an hour. Got Mildred to volunteer for the historical photo display and convinced Ruth to organize the kids' sandcastle competition."

"The Harbor Ladies are actually listening to her."

"More than listening. They like her." Jan refilled a nearby customer's coffee, then added, "Town's buzzing about how she saved the dock supplies during the storm. People respect someone who'll ruin a pair of expensive shoes to protect what matters."

He watched Cassidy gesture animatedly as she explained her vision for the recipe competition. Her hair was pulled back with a loose clip instead of her usual sleek style, and she wore shorts and a simple cotton shirt rather than the designer blazers she'd arrived in. She looked comfortable. She looked happy.

She looked nothing like the rigid, over-caffeinated executive who'd marched into that first committee meeting with a color-coded presentation and an attitude sharp enough to cut glass.

"I should probably interrupt before they rope her into running the entire town," he said.

Jan laughed. "Too late. Sally already asked if she'd help with the Christmas parade."

But then, she wouldn't be here at Christmas, would she? He pushed the thought away and made his way through the crowded coffee shop, catching fragments of conversation about fishing regulations and tourist season and whether the Johnsons would finally fix their dock before someone got hurt. The familiar rhythm of small-town life that had always grounded him.

"Bryan!" Cassidy spotted him and waved. "Perfect timing. We were just talking about the food vendors."

The Harbor Ladies turned their collective attention his way. Dorothy fixed him with a look that probably meant he was about to be volunteered for something.

"Your mother's clam chowder recipe," Dorothy said. It wasn't a question. "It needs to be part of the Heritage Recipe Competition."

"Mom would love that," Bryan said. "But she'd probably want to enter it properly, not get special treatment."

"Smart woman." Dorothy nodded with approval, then gathered her things. "We'll leave you two to discuss the menu planning. Cassidy, dear, send me those competition rules by Friday."

The four women departed in a wave of floral perfume and satisfied murmurs. Cassidy stared after them with an expression somewhere between triumph and disbelief.

"Did Dorothy just call me 'dear'?"

"You've been officially adopted." He slid into the chair across from her, grinning. "Congratulations. There's no escape now."

"I'm not sure I want to escape." She glanced down at her phone, where her notes app was filled with lists and ideas. "They know so much about this town. The stories they told about past festivals and about why certain traditions matter. It's incredible."

Something shifted inside him as he watched her scroll through her notes with genuine enthusiasm. This wasn't the polished professional executing a marketing strategy. This was someone who actually cared.

"I wanted to ask you something," he said. "We're doing a taste test tonight at the Sandpiper. Menu planning for the festival food. I thought you might want to be there. You know, since you're co-chair and all."

She looked up. "A taste test?"

"My family's been making the same dishes for three generations. We need to figure out what works for a festival setting versus the restaurant. Smaller portions, easier to eat while walking, that kind of thing." He rubbed the back of his neck. *Why was this suddenly awkward?* "Mom's going to be there. And my sister, Lucy. It's casual. Just family and food."

"You want me to meet your mother?"

The way she said it made it sound like he'd proposed something far more significant than a menu tasting. Heat crept up his neck.

"She's going to be at the festival anyway," he said quickly. "And she keeps asking about the woman who rescued the supply tent in a thunderstorm. Might as well get the interrogation over with."

Cassidy smiled, and it transformed her whole face. Not the polished professional smile she'd worn at that first meeting, but something genuine and a little uncertain.

"I'd like that," she said. "What time?"

"Seven. Come hungry."

Bryan spent the afternoon second-guessing every decision he'd made in the last four hours. Why had he invited Cassidy to a family dinner? This was supposed to be a working relationship. Professional. Focused on saving the festival and protecting the waterfront from developers like George Morton.

Except it hadn't felt professional when they'd worked together on her cottage porch last week, trading stories about their lives while planning vendor layouts. And it definitely hadn't felt professional when she'd texted him a photo of a terrible motivational poster she'd seen at the general store with the note: *Found your leadership style.*

He'd laughed so hard he'd nearly dropped his phone in the harbor.

"You're pacing." His mother appeared in the doorway of the Sandpiper's kitchen, wiping her hands on her apron. "What's wrong?"

"Nothing's wrong."

"You only pace when something's bothering you." She studied him with the x-ray vision that all mothers seemed to possess. "Is this about the festival?"

"The festival's fine. Great, actually. Cassidy's got sponsors lined up, the Harbor Ladies are helping with volunteers, and we've already got twice as many vendor applications as last year."

"Cassidy." His mother's expression shifted into something that made Bryan immediately suspicious. "The woman you invited to dinner tonight."

"It's not dinner. It's a menu tasting. For work."

"Mmhmm." She turned back to the stove, but he could hear the smile in her voice. "I made the clam chowder. And the grouper. And the key lime pie."

"Mom."

"What? You said taste test. I'm testing." She glanced over her shoulder. "Does this Cassidy have any food allergies I should know about?"

"I don't think so."

"You don't think so, or you don't know?"

Bryan pulled out his phone and texted Cassidy. *Any food allergies?*

Her response came immediately. *No. Why?*

My mother's asking.

Tell her I eat everything. And that I'm looking forward to meeting her.

He showed his mother the message. She read it, then patted his cheek like he was twelve years old.

"I like her already," she said.

He glanced at the back room one more time. The Sandpiper's back room had exposed brick walls, vintage fishing photographs, and a long wooden table that had hosted everything from family dinners to town council meetings. Bryan had set six places, then removed three, then put them back. Finally, he'd settled on four: himself, Mom, his sister Lucy, and Cassidy.

Casual. Professional. Definitely not a date.

He walked out to the main restaurant when the door opened. Cassidy stood in the entrance, backlit by the sunset over the Gulf. She'd changed into a soft blue dress that made her eyes look even brighter, and she held a bottle of wine like a peace offering.

"I wasn't sure if I should bring something," she said. "But I figured wine was safe."

"You didn't have to do that."

"I wanted to." She stepped inside and looked around the restaurant with obvious appreciation. The dinner rush was in full swing, so the main room was filled with chatter. She stepped closer. "Bryan, this place is beautiful."

He tried to see it through her eyes. The weathered wooden tables, the nautical decor that was probably twenty years out of style, and the slightly crooked floorboards that no one had bothered to fix because they'd been that way since the building was constructed.

"It's old," he said.

"It's authentic." She walked to the wall of photographs, studying the black-and-white images of fishing boats and harbor scenes. "Is this your grandfather?"

Bryan joined her at the photo she'd indicated. His grandfather stood on the deck of a shrimp boat, sun-weathered and grinning, holding up the day's catch.

"That's him. Took that boat out every morning for forty years."

"You look like him."

"I'll take that as a compliment."

"You should." She turned to face him, and they were suddenly very close in the quiet restaurant. "He looks happy."

"He loved the work. Even when it was hard, even when the catch was terrible, he loved being out on the water." He shoved his hands in his pockets. "I always thought I'd do the same. Take over the boat, keep the tradition going."

"But you ended up here instead."

"Someone had to run the restaurant. My cousin does most of the fishing now. I still try to get out three or four mornings a week, but fishing's not what it used to be. Regulations, quotas, and environmental changes. Some days it feels like the Gulf's trying to tell us our time is over."

The words came out heavy, more serious than he should probably have been. She reached out and touched his arm, a brief gesture of understanding that somehow steadied him.

"For what it's worth," she said quietly, "I think your grandfather would be proud of what you're doing. Protecting his legacy, keeping the restaurant going, and fighting for this community."

Before he could respond, his sister came out of the kitchen, balancing a tray on her hip. "You better get in there. Mom's getting antsy. She wants to know if you're going to make Cassidy stand in the dining room all night."

"Cassidy, this is my sister, Lucy."

"Nice to meet you."

"Nice to meet you too." Lucy glanced into the dining room. "Gotta go. Need to run this order over to table eight." She gave a little grin. "Good luck."

Cassidy turned to him. "Good luck? Luck with what?"

"The upcoming inquisition by my mom." He winked at her.

He led her to the back room, where his mother had already started bringing out dishes. She rearranged the table, and it looked nothing like the casual menu tasting he had planned. His mother had gone all out.

"You must be Cassidy." His mother wiped her hands and pulled Cassidy into a hug before Bryan could make proper introductions. "I'm Mona."

Lucy came into the room, and his mom said, "You've met Lucy, Bryan's baby sister."

Lucy rolled her eyes. "Mom, I'm not a baby, I'm thirty-five years old."

"You'll always be my baby." His mom bobbed her head with authority.

Hadn't his sister learned by now not to argue with their mother?

"Oh, you brought wine. That was thoughtful. Lucy, get some wine glasses for us." His mother stepped back to study Cassidy. "Bryan says you saved the dock supplies during the storm."

"I helped secure a tent. Bryan did most of the work."

"That's not how I heard it. Jan said you were out there in heels, wrestling support poles across the pier while lightning struck all around."

"Jan might have exaggerated slightly."

"Jan never exaggerates." Mona gestured to the table. "Sit, sit. Let's eat before everything gets cold."

Bryan held out a chair for Cassidy, earning a surprised smile that made his pulse kick up for no good reason. This was a working dinner, a professional collaboration. Nothing more.

Except his mother had made all his favorite dishes, and Lucy kept shooting him knowing looks, and Cassidy fit into the chaos of his family like she'd always been there.

"This is incredible," Cassidy said after her first taste of the clam chowder. "Mrs. Lucas, this is the best chowder I've ever had."

"Mona, please. And thank you, dear. It's my grandmother's recipe. She taught me when I was just a young girl." His mother ladled more into Cassidy's bowl despite her protests. "Bryan says you're from the city. Do you cook?"

"Not really. I'm usually too busy working to make real meals." Cassidy paused, then added more quietly, "Or I was. Before."

Lucy, bless her complete lack of filter, immediately asked, "Before what?"

"Lucy," Bryan warned.

"It's okay." Cassidy set down her spoon and met Lucy's curious gaze. "I had a bit of a... problem... at work. During a big presentation. Basically fell apart. My company put me on a mandatory sabbatical to recover."

The admission hung in the air. Bryan's mother and sister exchanged glances, and he braced himself for awkward sympathy or, worse, pity.

Instead, his mom reached over and patted Cassidy's hand.

"Good," she said firmly. "Any company that works someone until they collapse should be ashamed of themselves. And any woman brave enough to admit she needs a break deserves respect, not judgment."

Cassidy's eyes went suspiciously bright. "Thank you."

"Now eat. You're too thin. When's the last time you had a proper meal?"

Bryan watched Cassidy eat, genuinely enjoying the meal. She asked Mona about the grouper seasoning, laughed at Lucy's stories about tourist mishaps at the harbor, and somehow made his overbearing family seem almost normal.

"So," Lucy said as his mom brought out the key lime pie, "what do you think of our brother?"

Bryan nearly choked on his water. "Lucy."

"What? I'm just asking. You two are working together. I want to know if he's being a stubborn pain in the..."

His mom shot Lucy a stern look.

"A pain at committee meetings like he is at family dinners."

"He's been wonderful," Cassidy said. "Passionate about the festival, protective of the town's history, willing to compromise when it matters."

"That doesn't sound like Bryan at all." Lucy grinned. "Are we talking about the same person?"

"Okay, that's enough." Bryan pointed his fork at his sister. "You're supposed to make me look good, not destroy my reputation."

"Your reputation can handle it."

They stayed long past the tasting, talking and laughing while Mona kept refilling plates and Lucy told increasingly embarrassing stories about his childhood. Cassidy fit into the conversation like she'd known them for years instead of hours, asking questions and sharing her own stories about growing up in a small town in Indiana with a mom who worked part-time to help pay the bills.

"She sounds like a good mom," his mother said.

Cassidy frowned. "She is, though I spent most of my adult life trying to prove I was nothing like her." She pushed her pie around her plate. "She chose a simple life in a small town. I chose corporate ambition in the city. I thought I was so much smarter, so much more successful."

"And now?" he asked quietly.

She looked up, and her smile was sad and honest. "Now I'm not sure I know what success actually means."

"I think we each have to make our own definition of success," his mother said as she stood and started clearing plates. Lucy helped, leaving Bryan and Cassidy alone at the table. Through the windows, the Gulf stretched dark and vast under a scatter of stars.

"Thank you for inviting me," Cassidy said. "Your family is wonderful."

"They're loud, nosy, and completely lacking in boundaries."

"They love you. That's obvious." She traced the rim of her water glass. "I can't remember the last time I had a meal like this. With people who actually care about each other, who make time to be together even when they're busy."

He thought about all the meals he'd eaten at this table. Sunday dinners after church, birthdays, holidays, random Tuesday nights when his mother decided she wanted everyone together. He'd taken the easy comfort of family and tradition for granted.

"You're lonely," he said. It came out more as an observation than a question.

Cassidy didn't deny it. "I have colleagues, networking contacts, and people I see at industry events. But friends? Real friends?" She shook her head. "I've been too busy climbing the ladder to notice I was climbing it alone."

"You're not alone anymore." The words came before he could think better of them. "You've got the Harbor Ladies, Winnie, and the festival committee." He paused. "Me."

She met his eyes, and a strong current pulled between them. Not the hostility from their first meeting, not the wary truce from the storm, but something warmer and more dangerous.

"Bryan—"

"We should probably talk about the vendor

contracts," he said quickly, before whatever was happening could become something he'd have to acknowledge. "I pulled together the applications from last year. We can use them as a starting point and see who else we can get."

If Cassidy was disappointed by the subject change, she didn't show it. She pulled out her phone and opened her notes app, and they fell back into the comfortable rhythm of work.

But later, after she'd left and he was cleaning up the back room, he found himself thinking about the way she'd laughed at Lucy's jokes and the way she'd eaten seconds of his mother's cooking.

He thought about the way she'd looked at him when he'd said she wasn't alone.

He was in *serious* trouble.

CHAPTER 14

The knock on her cottage door pulled Cassidy away from the spreadsheet she'd been updating. She'd been cross-referencing vendor quotes with the festival budget, but her mind kept drifting to the dinner at The Sandpiper and the way Bryan had looked at her across the table.

She opened the door to find two women she'd seen around the lighthouse cottages standing on her porch.

"We heard you're running the festival," one woman said, holding out her hand. "I'm Emily, and this is Melissa."

"Co-chairing," Cassidy corrected automatically.

"Same thing." The other woman—Melissa, was it?—shifted her camera bag to her other shoulder. "We thought you might need help."

She blinked. Help. People kept offering that here. The concept still felt foreign.

"Come in." She stepped back to let them pass.

Emily settled onto the couch while Melissa prowled the room, eyeing the light through the windows with the critical assessment of someone who saw the world in exposures and compositions.

"What did you have in mind?" she asked.

"I could set up a photo booth," Melissa said. "I've got the equipment. Could do instant prints, maybe a digital share option too."

"That's actually perfect." She grabbed her notebook. "We need more interactive elements. Something that creates memories people want to share."

"I was thinking I could paint some backgrounds," Emily added. "Instagram-worthy stuff with the festival name. Might not help much this year, but when people post photos later, it spreads awareness for next time."

She paused mid-note. Next time. Emily was thinking about the festival's future, not just the immediate event.

"That would be incredible," she said. "Both of those ideas. Thank you."

"We want to do whatever we can to help. Just ask if you need anything else."

"That's very kind of you."

"We're neighbors." Emily shrugged like it was

obvious. "This is what we do." She got up and headed toward the door. Cassidy stood with them on the front porch. A man was working on one of the other cottages, replacing a section of railing. She'd seen him around but never spoken to him.

"Who's that?" Cassidy gestured toward the man with the tools.

"Cliff." Emily followed her gaze. "Winnie's nephew. He keeps to himself mostly."

"Unless he's telling me where I can and can't take photographs," Melissa muttered.

Emily laughed. "You two are going to have to work that out someday."

They wandered off toward their own cottages, and Cassidy stood there taking in the scene with the lighthouse rising against the blue sky. The neat cottages were arranged like protective arms around the garden, and the sound of waves drifted in the air..

All these people. Sally, Jan, the Harbor Ladies, and Bryan's family. And now Emily and Melissa. They'd woven her into their lives so easily, like she'd always belonged here.

Her phone buzzed in her pocket.

Everything okay, sweetie?

Her mother. Again. The second text this week asking the same careful question.

She stared at the message. Her mother had been asking variations of that question for months now. Maybe years. Are you sleeping? Are you eating? When was the last time you took a real day off?

Questions Cassidy had deflected with reassurances and the occasional white lie.

She looked at the phone in her hand, then at the lighthouse, and finally at the garden where she'd sat with Winnie drinking tea and talking about things that mattered.

Before she could second-guess the impulse, she pressed the call button.

Her mother answered on the second ring. "Cassidy? Are you all right?"

"I'm fine, Mom." She settled onto a chair on the porch. "I just wanted to talk."

Silence stretched across the line. Her mother was probably checking to make sure she'd texted the right number.

"That's wonderful, honey. How's Florida?"

"It's good. Different." She traced the edge of the wooden bench. "I'm helping with a town festival."

"A festival? That doesn't sound very restful."

"It's not work work. It's just helping the community." The words felt strange in her mouth.

"Tell me about it."

So Cassidy did. She talked about the festival, the committee meetings, and the Harbor Ladies. She mentioned The Sandpiper and Bryan's family, carefully keeping her tone neutral when she mentioned Bryan.

"You sound happy," her mother said quietly.

She opened her mouth to deflect, to make a joke about Florida sunshine or small-town charm. But she stopped.

"I think I might be," she admitted. "A little."

"Good. That's good, sweetheart." Her mother's voice went soft. "I've been worried about you for a long time."

"I know." Cassidy watched Cliff gather his tools and head toward Driftwood Cottage. "I'm sorry I don't call more."

"You're busy building your career. I understood that."

"Too busy." The admission came easier than she expected. "I let work become everything."

"I'm glad you're taking this break."

"I am, too, Mom. I am too."

They talked for another twenty minutes. Easy conversation about nothing and everything. Her mother's garden. The book club drama. The neighbor's new puppy. Normal things Cassidy had been too busy to discuss for years.

When she finally hung up, the sun was lower in the sky. Golden light slanted across the courtyard, turning everything warm and soft. She went back into the cottage. Her laptop sat open on the coffee table inside. She could see the email notification count from here. Forty-three new messages since this morning.

She used to check every hour. Every thirty minutes. Every time her phone buzzed.

Now she looked at that number and felt nothing but tired.

She closed the laptop without reading a single message.

The beach was quiet when she reached it. Cassidy slipped off her sandals and let her feet sink into the sand still warm from the day's sun. She walked toward the water, letting the waves chase her toes.

A pelican swooped low over the surf. She'd learned to identify them now. Pelicans and herons and the tiny sandpipers that raced along the tideline.

When had she learned those things? When had she stopped seeing the beach as scenery and started noticing the details?

She thought about Steve Hodges and the Phillips account. The career she'd built over years of eighty-hour weeks, skipped vacations, and relationships sacrificed at the altar of the next promotion.

That life felt impossibly far away, like something that had happened to a different person.

"Winnie said I might find you here."

She turned to find Bryan walking across the sand toward her. He'd changed out of his restaurant clothes into shorts and a faded t-shirt. His feet were bare.

They stood there watching the waves roll in. The silence felt comfortable instead of awkward. When had that changed?

"I talked to my mom today," Cassidy finally said. "Actually talked. For almost half an hour."

"That's good, right?"

"I haven't done that in years. I was always too busy." She dug her toes deeper into the sand. "She said I sounded happy. And I am." She glanced at him. "But my sabbatical ends in six weeks."

"Right. Of course." He looked out at the water. "Your real life is waiting. You have a career. A successful one."

"I don't know about that. I had a breakdown in front of forty people during a client presentation." The words came out flat. "My boss forced me to take leave because I couldn't function anymore. That's not success."

He turned to face her fully. "What do you want, Cassidy?"

She looked at the lighthouse rising against the darkening sky and the cottages with warm lights starting to glow from their windows. She looked at the man standing beside her with sand on his feet and concern in his eyes.

"I want to finish the festival," she said slowly. "I want to help make it something the town can be proud of. Something that honors what it's always been while making it sustainable for the future."

"That's five and a half weeks away."

"I know."

"And then what?"

The question hung between them like the suspended moment before a wave breaks.

"I don't know," she admitted.

Something shifted in Bryan's expression. Relief maybe. Or hope. He looked like he wanted to say something, but instead he just nodded.

"The vendor contracts came through," he said. "For the food trucks. We're cleared for six spots along the waterfront."

"That's great." She pulled her professional mask back into place. Easier to talk about logistics than whatever was happening between them. "Did you get the insurance documentation?"

"Sent it to your email an hour ago."

"I haven't checked my email today."

He raised an eyebrow. "At all?"

"At all." She said it like a confession, like admitting to a crime.

Bryan's mouth lifted into a smile. "The Harbor Ladies would be proud."

"They terrify me."

"They're supposed to. That's how you know they like you."

She laughed. The sound felt easy and natural.

"I should get back," Bryan said, but he didn't move. "Early morning at the restaurant."

"Right. Of course."

Neither of them walked away.

The sun was almost gone now, just a rim of gold on the horizon. The first stars were starting to appear overhead.

"Cassidy." His voice was soft. "I'm glad you're here. In Starlight Shores. Even if it's temporary."

Her heart did a little somersault. "Me too."

He smiled then, that warm, genuine smile that made his whole face change.

"Goodnight, Cassidy."

"Goodnight."

She watched him walk back across the beach toward town. His figure grew smaller against the last light until he disappeared around the bend.

Cassidy stood there alone with the waves and the cooling sand beneath her feet.

Six weeks until her sabbatical ended.

Six weeks that suddenly felt both infinite and desperately short.

She turned back toward Heron Cottage. Her laptop waited inside with its forty-three unread emails. Her old life calling her back.

But for tonight, she was here. With people who'd become friends. With a man whose smile made her forget about career trajectories and five-year plans.

She climbed the steps to her porch and paused with her hand on the door. She could see the lighthouse beam beginning its slow rotation, constant and steady.

CHAPTER 15

Winnie sat in Sally's cramped office behind the main general store floor, watching her oldest friend sort through the week's receipts. The small space was cluttered with inventory lists and vintage photographs of Starlight Shores, including one of Sally's grandfather standing beside Winnie's grandfather at the old dock.

"You're quiet today." Sally set down her pen and studied Winnie over the top of her reading glasses. "More quiet than usual, anyway."

Winnie traced the rim of her coffee mug. Through the office doorway, she could see customers browsing the aisles, their voices creating a low hum of activity. She'd come here seeking the comfort of Sally's welcoming presence, but the thoughts she had been wrestling with taunted her.

Sally looked at her. "Spill it."

"What?"

"Whatever is bothering you. After all these years, I can tell when you're trying to sort something out."

Winnie's lips curved into a small smile. Her friend knew her too well. She sighed. "Cassidy found something in the lighthouse archives. A photograph."

Sally's hands stilled on the papers. "What kind of photograph?"

"My grandfather with some men." She paused, choosing her words carefully, even here, even with Sally. "Academic consultants, according to the label. They were standing around equipment that looked too sophisticated for standard lighthouse operations."

"What did you tell her?"

"That my grandfather was dedicated to preservation, and he sought expert advice on maintaining the light." She had delivered that practiced explanation smoothly to Cassidy, her voice calm and matter-of-fact. She shrugged. "I was vague."

Sally removed her glasses and set them on the desk. Sally only put away her glasses when she was about to say something important, something she wanted Winnie to see clearly in her eyes.

"But we know there was something going on at the lighthouse all those years, don't we?"

The question hung between them, gentle but unrelenting. She looked down at her coffee, watching the surface ripple slightly from the vibration of someone's footsteps in the main store. How many times over the decades had she deflected similar questions? How many conversations had she steered away from the truth she herself only partially understood?

She nodded.

Sally leaned back in her chair, and it creaked softly. "Your father never told you the whole story."

"No. He said some things were better left in the past. That knowledge could become a burden I didn't need to carry. He said he'd explain when the time was right."

"But he died, and you've been carrying it anyway." Sally's voice held no judgment, only the understanding of someone who'd watched Winnie shoulder invisible weights for fifty years. "The not-knowing weighs just as much as knowing would."

She thought of the logbooks with their careful notations, the financial records that never quite added up, and the modifications to the lighthouse structure that served purposes she could only guess at. Her father had been meticulous in his duties, precise in his record-keeping. But there were gaps in those records, deliberate blank spaces where information should have been.

"I feel like my grandfather and father both

believed they were protecting something important, something bigger than themselves," she said slowly.

"And you've been protecting whatever that was ever since."

"I've been protecting the lighthouse. That's what my father asked of me. Keep it standing. Keep it private. Don't let anyone dig too deep into its history."

Sally was quiet for a moment, her expression thoughtful. Through the doorway, Winnie could hear Jan from Harbor Brew chatting with a customer about the upcoming festival, her cheerful voice a reminder that life in Starlight Shores continued its normal rhythms regardless of old secrets.

"You know what I think?" Sally finally said. "I think your father was trying to protect you, not just the lighthouse."

She ran the statement through her mind. She'd never considered it quite that way before. She'd always assumed her father's reticence was about duty, about maintaining operational security even decades after whatever operations had ceased. But what if it had been simpler than that? What if he'd simply wanted to spare his daughter from complicated truths?

"Maybe." Winnie's voice was soft.

"But now you want to know what was going on?"

A deep sigh slipped out. "I'm not sure I want to find out."

"Why not?"

The question was so quintessentially Sally. Straightforward and practical, cutting through layers of hesitation to the heart of the matter. Winnie loved and occasionally resented her friend's ability to do that.

"Because what if the truth changes how I see everything?" She set down her coffee mug, her fingers aching slightly. "The lighthouse has been my life, Sally. My purpose. What if I learn that purpose was built on something I can't reconcile? Something that makes me question whether all those years of service meant what I thought they meant?"

Sally reached across the desk and covered Winnie's hand with her own. Her palm was warm, her grip firm. They'd held hands like this countless times over decades of friendship, through storms both literal and metaphorical.

"Or what if the truth makes you realize your service meant even more than you knew?" Sally squeezed gently. "What if your grandfather and your father were protecting something genuinely important, and you've been honoring that legacy all these years without even knowing its full scope?"

Winnie hadn't considered that possibility. She'd been so focused on the fear of disillusionment that she hadn't imagined the alternative. What if the secrets weren't shameful but necessary? What if the careful discretion wasn't about hiding wrongdoing but about safeguarding something vital?

"I don't know how to find out," she admitted. "The records my father left are incomplete. Deliberately so, I think. And anyone who might have known the full story is long gone."

"Not necessarily." Sally released Winnie's hand and picked up her glasses again, settling them back on her nose. "There's someone who might know. Or at least know where to look for answers."

Winnie's heart gave an uncomfortable thump. She knew exactly who Sally meant. She'd been deliberately not thinking about him since the moment Cassidy had shown her that photograph, because thinking about him inevitably led to other thoughts and other memories she'd spent decades keeping carefully locked away.

"Sam," Winnie said quietly.

"Sam," Sally confirmed.

She stood abruptly, her chair scraping against the worn linoleum. She moved to the small window that looked out onto the alley behind the store. A delivery truck was unloading boxes, the driver whistling tunelessly. Such ordinary activity. Normal life continued while her carefully maintained composure threatened to crack.

"I'm not ready to talk to Sam."

"When will you be ready?" Sally's voice held a

gentle challenge. "Another month? Another year? Another decade?"

"I don't know." Winnie pressed her palm against the cool glass. "It's been so long, Sally. What would I even say to him?"

"How about the truth?" Sally shuffled papers, returning to her receipts with the air of someone who'd said her piece and would leave the decision where it belonged. "You could tell him you've spent almost fifty years wondering if you made the right choice when your father told you to break up with Sam. When your father said that it was important to the Lockhart legacy and the lighthouse. And you did as your father asked."

She closed her eyes. Sally knew her too well. They'd been friends too long for pretense.

Winnie finally turned from the window. Sally watched her with the expression she wore when she was worried about someone she loved. It was the same look she'd given Winnie years ago when Winnie had chosen the lighthouse over Sam, duty over possibility.

"I hurt him," Winnie said quietly. "When he asked me to leave with him, to let someone else take over the lighthouse. I chose my father's wishes over a future with him."

"You were twenty-three years old with a father who'd just asked you to carry on a responsibility you barely understood." Sally's voice was firm. "You made the choice you thought you had to make. That doesn't mean you have to keep making it for the rest of your life."

"My father needed me to help run the lighthouse."

"Your father loved you and wanted you to be happy." Sally stood, moving around the desk to stand beside Winnie. "I knew Robert Lockhart. He was a good man who carried heavy burdens. I don't think he would have wanted you to sacrifice everything for those burdens."

"He asked me to protect the lighthouse."

"He asked you to be its keeper." Sally's hand found Winnie's shoulder. "Not its prisoner."

The words landed like a stone in still water, sending ripples through assumptions Winnie had held for decades. She'd always thought of her role as keeper in terms of duty and obligation. The idea that it might have been something different, something that allowed for a life beyond the lighthouse's walls, felt both liberating and terrifying.

"Cassidy is curious," Winnie said, changing the subject because the other one had grown too large. "She's not going to stop wondering about that photograph. About the discrepancies in the records."

Sally accepted the shift without comment. "She's a problem-solver by nature. It's what makes her good at her work."

"I don't want her digging into things she doesn't understand. That I don't understand."

"Then get help to understand." Sally moved back to her desk, but her eyes remained on Winnie. "Or find someone who can."

There it was again. The suggestion hung in the air between them like morning mist over the harbor. Sam could possibly help her understand the lighthouse's history. His father had been friends with her father until they had a falling out. Sam was probably the only person left alive who might have both the knowledge and the discretion to navigate the complicated truth.

"I'll think about it," Winnie said.

Winnie picked up her coffee mug, found it empty, and set it back down. Through the doorway, she could see the general store's familiar aisles, the same layout Sally's grandfather had established seventy years ago. Some things remained constant. Some traditions were worth preserving.

But not all preservation was healthy. Sometimes holding too tightly to the past meant losing the possibility of a future.

"The photograph Cassidy found," Winnie said slowly. "My grandfather is standing with three men in suits. There's radio equipment in the background that definitely wasn't standard lighthouse gear."

"What do you think it was for?"

"I don't know." Winnie's shoulders felt heavy.

"Communications, maybe. Monitoring. My father always said the lighthouse's history was complicated and the official records didn't tell the whole story."

"And you never pushed him for details."

"He was my father." Her voice held a lifetime of loyalty. "If he said something was better left alone, I trusted his judgment."

Sally nodded slowly. "But now Cassidy is asking questions. And Emily found that journal in Starfish Cottage. There are a lot of questions."

"Yes, there are," Winnie agreed.

Winnie knew Sally was right. She'd known it from the moment Cassidy had shown her that photograph. Sam might be the key to understanding her family's legacy, to finally knowing the full truth about the lighthouse she'd devoted her life to protecting.

But she wasn't ready to reach out to him, and she wasn't sure she was ready to learn the truth.

CHAPTER 16

Cassidy stood on the dock at six in the morning, watching Bryan prepare the *Mary Catherine* for departure. The sun was barely up, and the sky was tinted with shades of pale coral and gold. She'd worn sensible shoes this time. Boat shoes, actually, purchased from the general store after Sally had informed her that heels and boats didn't mix. While she was in town, she'd picked up some shorts and a couple of t-shirts, not that she'd ever been a t-shirt type of person.

"You're here early." Bryan looked up from the rope he was coiling. "Coffee's in the cabin if you need it."

"I've had two cups already." She stepped carefully from the dock to the boat, pleased when she didn't stumble. "What are we doing exactly?"

"Testing the boat parade route." He secured the

rope and moved to the helm. "I want to make sure the timing works before we commit to it in all the promotional materials you're designing."

She settled onto the bench near the cabin as the engine rumbled to life. The harbor was quiet at this hour. A few other fishing boats were heading out, and their captains raised hands in silent greeting as they passed. Bryan returned each gesture with the easy familiarity of someone who'd known these people his entire life.

They cleared the harbor entrance, and the Gulf opened before them. The water was calm, with barely a ripple disturbing its surface. She breathed in the salt air and felt a simple peace flow through her.

"We'll follow the proposed route." Bryan adjusted their heading. "Start at the harbor mouth, loop around the lighthouse point, and come back along the beach. Should take about forty-five minutes at parade speed."

"And at regular speed?"

"Twenty minutes. But we're not in a hurry." He glanced at her. "Unless you have somewhere to be?"

She thought of her color-coded sabbatical schedule, abandoned weeks ago in a drawer, and the urgent emails still piling up in her inbox, unread.

"No," she said. "I don't have anywhere to be."

They motored along in comfortable silence. She watched the shoreline slide past with beach cottages, the lighthouse rising white against the morning sky, and the pier where she'd wrestled that tent in the storm. Everything looked different from the water. Smaller somehow, but also more connected.

"Can I ask you something?" Bryan kept his eyes on the water ahead. "What made you agree to help with the festival? The real reason."

She could have deflected and given him the polished answer about professional development or portfolio building. But something about the morning, the quiet boat, and the way he'd asked without looking at her made honesty feel easier.

"I was afraid of disappearing," she said. "At work, I mean. Steve, a co-worker, was taking over my accounts. My boss was making decisions without me. I could feel myself being erased while I sat in that cottage doing nothing." She wrapped her arms around herself despite the growing warmth. "The festival gave me something to do. Proof I still existed."

Bryan slowed the boat slightly, adjusting their course around a channel marker. "And now?"

"Now I'm not sure." She watched a pelican plunk down on the water. "I started this as a project. Something to put on my resume. But it's become something else."

"What?"

"I don't know. Something real maybe." She looked at him. "Does that make sense?"

"Yeah." He nodded slowly. "It makes sense."

The lighthouse was growing larger as they approached. She could see the cottages arranged around the courtyard and the keeper's quarters where Winnie probably already had coffee brewing.

Home. When had she started thinking of Heron Cottage as home instead of temporary housing?

"I'm terrified I'm going to fail," Bryan said suddenly. "The festival, the restaurant, the fishing business. All of it. I lie awake at night running numbers, trying to figure out how to make everything work." He shrugged. "And I can't."

She turned to face him fully. His jaw was set, and his hands gripped the wheel.

"I see my grandfather standing at that grill," he continued. "My father working the dining room. Three generations of Lucas men building something that mattered. And I'm the one who's going to lose it all because I can't figure out how to adapt fast enough."

"You're not going to lose it."

"You don't know that." He glanced at her, and the fear in his eyes was raw. "Morton's offer is still on the table. The bank is still deciding about my loan extension. One bad season, one health inspection violation, one festival that doesn't bring in enough revenue, and it all collapses."

She understood that fear. Had lived with its twin for years. The terror of not being enough, of failing to meet impossible standards, and disappointing everyone who'd invested in your success.

"What would you do?" she asked. "If you weren't afraid of failing?"

The question seemed to catch him off guard. He was quiet for a long moment, steering them around the lighthouse point. The beach opened up before them, stretching toward town. Empty this early except for a few joggers and someone walking a dog.

"I'd experiment more at the restaurant," he said slowly. "Try new dishes instead of sticking to the same menu we've had for twenty years. I'd take the boat out less and focus on making the restaurant sustainable. Maybe hire a real chef instead of relying on Mom and me." He paused. "I'd stop trying to do everything exactly the way it's always been done and figure out what actually works now."

"But you're afraid that would be disrespectful."

"Yeah." He cut the engine back to an idle, letting them drift. "Feels like admitting my grandfather and father were wrong, and that their way isn't good enough anymore."

"Or it's admitting that times change," she said. "That honoring their legacy means keeping the spirit of what they built alive, not preserving it in amber."

He looked at her and smiled gently. "Wise woman."

"I'm not wise. I'm just good at seeing other people's problems clearly." She laughed, but it came out hollow. "My own problems are a complete disaster."

"What are your problems?"

The question was genuinely curious. Just Bryan, asking because he wanted to know.

"I don't know who I am without a deadline," she admitted. "Without a project to complete, a client to impress, or a presentation to deliver. I've spent my adult life defining myself by what I accomplish. And when that was taken away, I just... dissolved, like I was never really there in the first place."

He turned off the engine completely. They drifted on the gentle current, the boat rocking slightly. The only sounds were water lapping against the hull and distant seagull cries.

"You're here right now," he said. "On this boat. Helping with this festival. That's real."

"But it's temporary. I have to go back eventually."

"Do you?"

The question hung between them, heavy with implications she wasn't ready to examine. Of course she had to go back. Her apartment was in Chicago. Her career, her entire professional identity, and the life she'd built over two decades. She couldn't just abandon all that because she'd had a nice few weeks in a small coastal town.

"I don't know," she said quietly.

He stood and moved to sit beside her on the bench. Not touching, but close enough that she could feel the warmth of him. They sat there watching the shoreline with the lighthouse standing watch over the harbor it had protected for generations.

"My grandfather used to say that the lighthouse's job was to show people where they were," he said. "Not where they should be. Not where they'd been. Just where they were right now, in this moment."

"That's lovely."

"He was talking about navigation. Helping ships find their position so they could chart their course. But I always thought it applied to life too." He turned to look at her. "You don't have to know where you're going yet. You just have to know where you are."

She met his eyes. They were warm and steady, the same gray-blue as the Gulf on a calm day.

"I'm on a boat," she said. "In Starlight Shores. With you."

"That's a good place to be."

The moment stretched between them, charged with possibility. She thought about leaning closer and closing that small distance. About what might happen if she did.

Bryan's phone buzzed, shattering the stillness. He pulled it from his pocket and frowned at the screen.

"Mom. The restaurant." He stood, already moving back to the helm. "I need to get back."

"Of course."

He started the engine, and they headed toward the harbor at a speed faster than parade pace. The moment was gone, but its echo remained. She could still feel the warmth of him beside her and his words settling into places that had been empty for too long.

They didn't talk on the return trip. He focused on navigating, and she watched the water slip past, but the silence felt full instead of awkward.

When they reached the dock, he secured the boat. She stepped onto the weathered planks.

"The route works," he said. "I estimate forty-three minutes at parade speed." He smiled. "You know, if they don't all cut their engines and talk for a bit. We should budget an hour to be safe."

"I'll update the schedule."

He climbed onto the dock beside her. They stood there in the strengthening sunlight, neither quite ready to return to the demands of the day.

"Thank you," she said. "For taking me out. For showing me the route."

"You're the co-chair. You needed to see it."

"I meant thank you for the conversation."

Something softened in his expression. "Yeah. Me too."

He walked toward town, and she headed back to the lighthouse. She stopped for a moment and turned to watch him go. He moved with the easy confidence of someone who knew every inch of this place, who belonged here so completely that the town and the man were inseparable.

She envied his certainty of belonging and the deep roots that connected him to generations of history and community.

But maybe, she thought as she climbed the steps to Heron Cottage, belonging wasn't something you were born into. Maybe it was something you built, day by day, connection by connection. Maybe she'd been building it here without even realizing it.

Inside the cottage, her laptop sat on the coffee table where she'd left it last night. She opened it and stared at her inbox. Sixty-two unread messages now. Steve's name appeared multiple times. Her boss had sent a check-in email. HR wanted to schedule her return-to-work meeting.

Her old life, calling her back.

She thought about what Bryan said about not knowing where you're going yet. You just have to know where you are.

She was in Heron Cottage, in Starlight Shores,

working on a festival that mattered to people she was starting to care about. She was living a life that looked nothing like the one she'd planned but felt more real than anything she had experienced in years.

She closed the laptop without reading a single email.

CHAPTER 17

The morning started well enough. Cassidy sat at Harbor Brew with her laptop, reviewing vendor contracts and feeling the quiet satisfaction of a project coming together. The festival timeline spreadsheet glowed on her screen, every task color-coded and assigned. She'd learned to balance the Harbor Ladies' traditional requirements with practical modern updates.

Jan refilled her coffee without being asked. "You look happy."

"Do I?" Cassidy glanced up from the spreadsheet.

"You've got that look people get when they're doing something they love." Jan topped off the mug. "It's nice to see."

After Jan moved to the next table, Cassidy sat with what Jan had said. Happy. That word kept coming up. Her corporate colleagues used words like driven, focused, and intense. Never happy.

Her phone buzzed with a text from Bryan. *Found three more food vendors who want in. Sending contracts now.*

She smiled as she typed back. *Perfect. We're at capacity for the pier section.*

The door opened, and a man in a pressed suit walked into Harbor Brew. He looked around the casual coffee shop as if he'd accidentally walked into the wrong establishment. Everything about him screamed business, from his expensive watch to his Italian shoes.

He spotted Cassidy and headed straight for her table.

"Ms. Wren?" He extended his hand. "George Morton, Oceanside Development. Do you have a few minutes?"

Every professional instinct she had developed over the years went on alert. She recognized a corporate pitch when she saw one coming.

"I'm working on the festival right now." She gestured to her laptop.

"Actually, that's exactly what I wanted to discuss." He pulled out the chair across from her without waiting for an invitation. "I understand you're co-chairing the Harbor Festival this year."

"That's right."

"I've been following the progress. Very impressive what you've accomplished in such a short time." He set a leather portfolio on the table. "The vendor lineup, the expanded programming, and the Heritage Recipe Competition. You've brought real professionalism to the event."

The compliment felt false. Cassidy closed her laptop slowly. "What can I do for you, Mr. Morton?"

"Please, call me George." He opened the portfolio and pulled out a folder. "Oceanside Development is very interested in supporting community initiatives in Starlight Shores. We believe the Harbor Festival represents an excellent opportunity for partnership."

"Partnership?"

"We'd like to be the festival's primary sponsor." He slid a paper across the table. "This is our proposed contribution."

She looked at the number written at the top of the page. Her breath caught. It was more than their entire current budget. More than she'd dared hope to raise from all local sponsors combined.

"That's very generous."

"We believe in investing in the communities where we operate." George's smile was practiced and professional. "The festival is an important tradition. We want to help ensure its success."

There it was. The word that always preceded the catch. She had sat through enough corporate pitches to know nothing came without strings attached.

"What would Oceanside expect in return?"

"Minimal branding. Very tasteful." He pulled out another document with glossy renderings of what the festival would look like with Oceanside's involvement. "We'd install branded archways at the main pier entrance, some banners along the waterfront, and recognition in all marketing materials as the main sponsor, of course."

She studied the renderings. The archways were massive. Sleek, modern structures that would completely change the character of the historic pier. The Oceanside logo was everywhere, overshadowing the festival's own identity.

"This is more than minimal branding."

"It's proportional to our investment." George's voice remained pleasant. "We're contributing significant resources. We deserve appropriate recognition."

She thought of Bryan and the way he'd talked about his grandfather grilling fish on the beach during the first festival. And Dorothy and her husband setting up vendor tents with their own hands. Of seventy-four years of community gathering around simple traditions.

These archways would turn all that into a corporate event.

"I appreciate the offer," she said carefully, "but

I'll need to discuss this with my co-chair and the committee."

"Of course." George pulled out his business card. "But I should mention that this offer has a time limit. We need to make our community investment decisions by the end of the week. If the festival doesn't fit our criteria, we'll redirect those funds elsewhere."

The deadline pressure. Another classic negotiation tactic. Create urgency to force a decision before the target could think too carefully.

"I understand." She took the card. "I'll be in touch."

After George left, she sat staring at the number on the proposal. With this money, they could afford professional sound equipment, along with most of her wishlist for the festival. They could make the festival bigger and more successful than it had been in a decade.

All it would cost was the festival's soul.

Her phone buzzed. Another text from Bryan. *Mom wants to know if you'd like to come to dinner Sunday. She's making roast beef.*

She looked at the message, then at the Oceanside proposal, then back at the message.

She picked up the proposal and walked to the trash can. She stood there for a long moment, the paper heavy in her hands. This was ill-advised and financially irresponsible. She was a marketing executive. She knew better than to turn down major sponsorship deals based on aesthetic concerns.

Except it wasn't about aesthetics. It was about protecting something that mattered to people she cared about.

She dropped the proposal in the trash and went back to her table.

She looked out Harbor Brew's window. Across the street, Sally was opening the general store, propping the door with the same wooden wedge her grandfather had probably used. The Harbor Ladies walked past in their usual formation, heading to their corner table. Bryan's truck was parked outside The Sandpiper, which meant he was already there working.

This was real life. These people, this town, and this festival that mattered more than attendance numbers or revenue projections.

Her corporate career waited for her like a well-tailored suit hanging in a closet, professional and appropriate. Maybe it was slightly uncomfortable but acceptable because that was the price of success.

Except Cassidy wasn't sure she wanted to wear that suit anymore.

She reopened her laptop and pulled up the festival budget. They were running lean but functional. Local sponsors had come through with smaller contributions. The Heritage Recipe Competition had generated excitement that didn't cost anything. They'd make it work without Oceanside's money.

They *had* to make it work without Oceanside's money.

Her phone rang. Unknown number. She almost didn't answer, but professional habit made her pick up.

"Ms. Wren? This is Kathleen Brown from the Gulf Coast Tourism Board. I heard about your Harbor Festival, and I'm very interested in featuring it in our summer destination guide."

She sat up straighter. "Really?"

"We're always looking for authentic coastal experiences to promote. Your festival sounds exactly like what we want to highlight. Small town charm, local traditions, that kind of thing." Kathleen's voice was warm and genuine. "Would you be interested in an interview? We could send a photographer to cover the event."

"That would be wonderful." She grabbed her notebook. "What information do you need?"

They talked for twenty minutes. Kathleen asked questions about the festival's history, the community involvement, and the traditions that made it special. She didn't mention target demographics or brand positioning. She just wanted to know what made the Harbor Festival worth visiting.

She found herself telling stories instead of reciting statistics. Sally's husband proposing at the festival. Bryan's grandfather grilling fish on the beach. The boat parade through the harbor and around the point with the boats all lit up with lights.

"This is perfect," Kathleen said when Cassidy finished. "Exactly the kind of authentic experience our readers are looking for. I'll send you a message, and we'll schedule the photographer."

After they hung up, she sat with her notebook open to the page where she'd scribbled notes during the call. The Gulf Coast Tourism Board had a readership of over a hundred thousand and a huge social media presence. Their endorsement would bring more visitors than any paid advertising campaign she could have designed.

And it wouldn't cost the festival a single dollar or a single piece of its identity.

She pulled out George Morton's business card and typed an email on her phone.

Mr. Morton,

Thank you for your generous sponsorship offer. After careful consideration, I've decided it's not the right fit for the Harbor Festival. We're committed to maintaining the event's traditional character, and your branding requirements would fundamentally change that.

Best regards,

Cassidy Wren

. . .

She hit send before she could second-guess herself.

Her corporate training screamed that she'd just made a terrible business decision. You didn't turn down major sponsors; you negotiated terms, found compromises, and made it work. That's what professionals did.

But maybe being professional wasn't always the same as doing the right thing.

"You look like you just made a big decision." Jan appeared with the coffee pot.

"I think I did." She held out her mug for a refill. "I'm just not sure if it was smart or foolish."

"In my experience, the smart decisions and the right decisions aren't always the same thing." Jan topped off the coffee. "The trick is figuring out which one you can live with."

The town square was alive with music and laughter. White string lights hung between the trees, swaying gently in the evening breeze. The gazebo glowed like a lantern in the center of it all, and a three-piece band played something bluesy and warm. People milled around picnic tables laden with donated food, their voices rising and falling in comfortable conversation.

Cassidy stood near the edge of the gathering and tried to remember the last time she'd attended a community event that wasn't a networking mixer. Her shoes sank slightly into the uneven ground. She was glad she'd forsaken her heels for flats.

"Cassidy!" Sally waved from a table near the gazebo. "Come try Dorothy's pecan pie before it's gone."

She smiled and waved back but stayed where

she was. The Harbor Ladies had outdone themselves with this fundraiser. Every detail reflected the authentic charm she'd been working so hard to preserve. No corporate logos. No slick branding. Just neighbors supporting neighbors.

Her phone buzzed in her clutch. She pulled it out and glanced at the screen. Another email from Steve Hodges with the subject line: *Phillips Pitch Update*. She swiped it away without reading it.

Three weeks ago, that email would have sent her into a spiral. Now it just felt distant. Like news from someone else's life.

"Impressive turnout."

She turned. Bryan stood a few feet away with his hands in his pockets. He wore khakis and a button-down shirt with the sleeves rolled to his elbows. His hair was still damp, like he'd showered right before coming.

"The Harbor Ladies did most of the heavy lifting," she said. "I just helped with the promotion."

"They told me you strong-armed the bakery into donating desserts."

"I negotiated. There's a difference."

His mouth twitched. Not quite a smile, but close. He looked past her toward the gazebo where couples had started dancing. His jaw tightened slightly. "I heard George Morton offered to sponsor the festival," he said.

The shift in his tone was immediate. Casual to guarded in three seconds flat.

She straightened her shoulders. "He did."

"And?"

"And I turned him down."

His gaze snapped back to her. His eyes were dark in the dim light, searching her face for something. Proof, maybe.

"You turned down that much money?" His voice was carefully neutral, but she heard the doubt underneath.

She'd been expecting this. The distrust and the assumption that she'd cave to the numbers because that's what corporate people did. A week ago, it would have stung. Now it just made her tired.

"Yes, Bryan. I turned it down." She kept her voice even. "Morton wanted aggressive branding. His corporate logo on everything. Oceanside banners at every entrance. Essentially, he wanted to buy the festival's identity."

"But the funding—"

"Would have come with strings attached that would have destroyed everything we've been working to preserve." She crossed her arms. "I'm not a fool. I know what his offer meant."

He studied her for another long moment. The music swelled behind them. Someone laughed, bright and unrestrained.

"I also got a call from Kathleen Brown at the

Gulf Coast Tourism Board. They want to feature the Starlight Harbor Festival in their destination guide, specifically in their authentic small-town events section. No cost to us, just exposure to thousands of potential visitors who are looking for what we're offering."

Something shifted in Bryan's expression. The tension in his shoulders eased slightly.

"That's the kind of partnership that makes sense," she continued. "The kind that highlights what's already special instead of trying to rebrand it into something marketable."

He nodded slowly. The distrust was fading from his eyes, replaced by something warmer that made her stomach flutter in a way she absolutely did not have time to analyze.

"I should have known better than to assume you'd sell out," he said quietly.

"You should have." She tried to sound stern, but a smile tugged at her lips. "But I'll forgive you this once."

"Generous of you."

"I'm a very generous person."

This time, he did smile. A smile that was full and genuine, the kind that crinkled the corners of his eyes. Her heart beat in a quick rhythm.

The song changed to something slower. More couples moved onto the makeshift dance floor near the gazebo.

He cleared his throat. "Would you want to dance?"

She blinked. "What?"

"Dance." He gestured toward the gazebo. "It's a fundraiser. There's music. People are dancing."

"I know what a dance is, Bryan."

"Then why are you stalling?"

Because dancing with him felt dangerous. Because every moment she spent in this town made her old life feel more like a costume she'd outgrown.

"I'm not stalling," she said. "I'm considering."

"Consider faster." He held out his hand.

She looked at his palm, calloused and scarred from years of hauling nets and fixing engines. Nothing like the soft, manicured hands of the executives she used to network with at corporate events.

She placed her hand in his.

The dance floor was crowded enough that they had to stand close. Bryan's hand settled on her waist, warm through the thin fabric of her dress. She rested her hand on his shoulder and tried to remember how to breathe normally.

"You're tense," he said.

"I'm not tense."

"Your shoulders are up by your ears."

She forced herself to relax. "Better?"

"Marginally."

They swayed to the music. She was acutely

aware of every point of contact between them. His hand on her waist. Her palm against his shoulder. Their joined hands between them.

This was fine. This was just a dance. People danced at fundraisers all the time. It didn't mean anything.

Except it did mean something. She knew it did.

"You're thinking too loud," he said as he smiled at her.

"I'm not thinking anything."

"Liar."

She looked up and found him watching her with an expression that was far too knowing. She wanted to deflect, make a joke, and change the subject to something safe like vendor contracts or parking logistics.

Instead, she said, "I'm thinking that this is nice."

His hand tightened slightly on her waist. "Yeah?"

"Yeah." The admission felt reckless. "I can't remember the last time I did something like this. Something that wasn't attached to an outcome or a goal."

"You're having fun without a productivity metric?"

"Apparently."

"Careful, Wren. People might think you're human."

She laughed. Actually laughed, light and surprised.

They turned in a slow circle. The Harbor Ladies passed by with knowing smiles. Cassidy caught Dorothy's eye and felt her cheeks warm.

"They're going to talk," she murmured.

"They're already talking," he said. "Have been since the committee meeting where you told me my marketing strategy was garbage."

"I did not say it was garbage."

"You said it was functionally invisible. That's worse."

"Well, it was. Invisible, I mean."

He grinned. "And now look at us. Dancing at the fundraiser for a festival you're organizing."

"You're helping too."

"I mostly argue with you." He grinned.

"True." She tilted her head. "But you come around eventually."

"Because you wear me down."

"Because I'm right."

He chuckled. "Also true."

The song shifted into something even slower. Couples drew closer together. Bryan's thumb traced along her waist, probably unconsciously.

This was a terrible idea. She was leaving in three more weeks. Her sabbatical would end, and she'd go back to Chicago. Back to her apartment and her career and the life she'd spent years building.

Except that life felt like it belonged to someone else now.

"You're doing it again," Bryan said.

"Doing what?"

"Thinking too loud."

She wanted to deny it, but what was the point? He could read her too easily now. Somewhere along the way, he'd learned to see past her carefully constructed walls.

"I'm just wondering if I'm going to regret this," she said honestly.

His expression grew serious. "The dance?"

"All of it." She met his eyes. "The festival. This town. You."

The word hung between them, heavy and terrifyingly true.

He was quiet for a long moment. When he spoke, his voice was rough. "Would regret be so bad?"

"What?"

"If you go back to Chicago and you regret leaving here." He pulled her infinitesimally closer. "At least you'd know you felt something. That's more than you had before."

The truth of it hit her squarely. She'd been numb for so long. Buried under deadlines and the constant pressure to prove she was indispensable.

Here, in this ridiculously wonderful small town with its struggling festival and stubborn fishermen, she'd started feeling again. Joy, frustration, and hope. All the messy, complicated emotions she'd been too busy to process.

"When did you get so smart?" she asked.

"I've always been smart. You were just too stubborn to notice."

She laughed again.

The song ended, and the band announced they were taking a short break. Couples began drifting away from the dance floor, but Bryan didn't let go of her hand.

"I'm going to get us drinks," he said. "Don't run away."

"Where would I go?"

"Your cottage. Your laptop. Chicago." His thumb brushed across her knuckles. "You have options."

"I'm not running."

"Good." He released her hand slowly, like he wasn't quite ready to let go. "I'll be right back."

She watched him navigate through the crowd toward the refreshment table. Sally caught his arm and said something that made him laugh. Marty clapped him on the shoulder. Bryan belonged here in a way she had never belonged anywhere.

"You two make a lovely couple."

Cassidy turned. Dorothy stood beside her with a knowing smile and a plate of pie.

"We're not a couple," she said automatically.

"Of course not." Dorothy's tone suggested she didn't believe that for a second.

"We're co-chairing the festival. That's all."

"Mmm-hmm." Dorothy took a bite of pie. "That's why you were looking at him like he hung the moon."

"I was not—"

"Honey, I've been watching people fall in love in this town for... well, a lot of years. I know what I'm seeing."

Fall in love. The words sent panic skittering through her.

"I'm leaving in three weeks," she said. "My sabbatical ends. I have a job waiting for me in Chicago."

"Do you want that job?"

The question was so simple and so direct. And Cassidy had no idea how to answer it.

Three months ago, she would have said yes without hesitation. Now? Now she wasn't sure.

"It's complicated," she said finally.

Dorothy patted her arm. "Life usually is, dear. But that doesn't mean the answer has to be."

She drifted away before Cassidy could respond, leaving her standing alone with thoughts that felt far too big for a town square fundraiser.

Bryan returned with two cups of lemonade. "You okay? You look like you're solving world hunger."

"Just thinking."

"About?"

About whether I'm making the biggest mistake of my life. About whether going back to Chicago means giving up something I didn't know I needed. About whether three weeks is enough time to figure out who I am when I'm not trying to prove anything.

"About how good the turnout is," she said instead. "The Harbor Ladies really delivered."

He studied her for a moment, and she knew he didn't believe her deflection. But he didn't push.

"They did," he agreed. "I think we might actually hit our fundraising goal."

"We'll exceed it." She took a sip of lemonade. Too sweet, but refreshing. "Kathleen from the tourism board is sending a photographer next week to get some preliminary shots. They want to promote the festival on their social media. We can share the posts."

"Look at you, always thinking marketing strategy."

"Don't sound so surprised."

"I'm not surprised." His voice softened. "I'm impressed."

The compliment wrapped around her like a warm blanket on a chilly night. She'd spent years chasing praise from clients and supervisors, always needing external validation to feel capable. But Bryan's approval felt different. It felt real.

The band returned to the gazebo and launched into something upbeat. Children ran shrieking past them, chasing each other around the picnic tables. Mayor West was deep in conversation with Captain Roy near the edge of the square.

"Thank you," she said suddenly. "For not writing me off as another corporate outsider trying to ruin everything."

"I definitely wrote you off at first."

"I know. I was there." She laughed.

He smiled. "But you proved me wrong. You kept showing up. You listened. You cared about getting it right."

"I still care about getting it right."

"I know." He shifted closer, just enough that their shoulders brushed. "That's why this is going to work."

She wanted to ask what *this* was. The festival? Their partnership? The fragile, terrifying thing growing between them?

But she didn't. Because some questions didn't have answers yet. Some things just had to unfold in their own time.

Bryan touched her elbow lightly. "Want to get out of here? Take a walk?"

She should probably stay, network with the

committee members, and thank the volunteers. Do the responsible, productive thing.

Instead, she said, "Yeah. I'd like that."

They slipped away from the fundraiser as the band played on. The music followed them down the street, fading gradually as they walked toward the water. Neither of them spoke, but the silence felt comfortable and natural.

The night air was warm and salt-sweet. Somewhere in the distance, she could hear waves meeting the shore. She didn't know what would happen in three weeks, but right now she wasn't going to worry about it. She slipped her hand into Bryan's.

CHAPTER 19

The week before the festival arrived with the kind of relentless momentum Cassidy used to thrive on. Vendor confirmations poured in. Permit approvals landed in her inbox. The volunteer schedule had finally stopped resembling a jigsaw puzzle of conflicts and impossible demands.

She should have felt triumphant. She did. And proud of herself that things were finally falling into place.

Her phone buzzed. Another email notification. She'd made the mistake of using her main business email account—force of habit—for some of the festival correspondence, which meant her carefully separated worlds now bled into each other with alarming frequency.

She opened it. A tourism board confirmation. Good news. She should forward it to Bryan.

The next email made her pause.

Steve Hodges. Subject line: *Quick Question.*

She deleted it without reading.

Two minutes later, another one arrived. Steve again. Subject line: *Following Up.*

"Unbelievable." She deleted that one too.

The third email came ten minutes later. Subject line: *URGENT.*

That wasn't like Steve. He specialized in casual undermining, not genuine emergencies. His whole strategy relied on making everything look effortless while he systematically dismantled her work behind the scenes.

She stared at the subject line. She could feel the old instinct rising inside her, the one that said ignoring urgent messages was irresponsible and she needed to at least know what crisis had erupted in her absence.

But she was on sabbatical. His emergencies weren't her problem anymore.

But her finger hovered over the email anyway.

She clicked.

Cass, I know you're off the grid, but I really need your help on the Phillips account. There's a situation with the demographic targeting, and I can't find your notes on the Q3 strategy pivot. Can you call me ASAP? I wouldn't ask if it wasn't critical.

She read it twice, searching for the trap. Steve never asked for help. He took credit, deflected blame, and occasionally lobbed passive-aggressive comments about how they had different approaches, but he didn't admit to needing assistance.

She closed the email and set her phone face down on the table.

Whatever was happening in Chicago, it wasn't her responsibility.

The phone rang, and she glanced at it. Unknown number, but the area code was Chicago.

Her hand reached for it automatically, years of corporate conditioning overriding common sense. She caught herself, pulled back, and let it go to voicemail.

Thirty seconds later, it rang again. Same number.

"For heaven's sake." She snatched it up. "Hello?"

"Cassidy. Finally." David Wilde's voice filled her ear with the kind of brisk authority that used to make her stand up straighter. "I've been trying to reach you for two days."

Her boss. Her actual boss, not Steve. The nausea hit immediately.

"David. Hi. I'm on sabbatical. I thought—"

"I know, I know. And normally I wouldn't interrupt your recovery time." He had the decency to sound slightly apologetic. "But we have a situation, and frankly, you're the only one who can fix it."

She walked to the window and watched Winnie move through the garden with unhurried grace. "What kind of situation?"

"The Phillips account is imploding. Steve completely misread the client's priorities and pitched them a strategy that's essentially the opposite of what they asked for. They're threatening to pull the contract."

A small, vindictive part of her wanted to laugh. Steve Hodges, the golden boy who'd been poaching her accounts and taking credit for her campaigns, had finally overextended himself.

"That's unfortunate," she said carefully.

"Unfortunate?" David's voice sharpened. "Cassidy, this is a multi-million-dollar account. I need you back in Chicago immediately."

The room tilted slightly. "You need me to come back early? From leave?"

"I need you to save this account. And when you do, I'm prepared to offer you Senior VP of Strategy. Corner office. Twenty percent raise. Full creative authority over client selection." He paused, letting the offer sink in. "This is everything we've discussed for your career trajectory. It's happening now instead of in three or four years."

Everything she'd worked for.

The title she'd been chasing since she became junior executive.

The validation that all those eighty-hour weeks

and missed dinners and sacrificed relationships had been worth it.

"How soon can you be here?" David pressed. "I can have a ticket waiting for you at Tampa International this afternoon."

Her reflection stared back at her from the window, superimposed over the courtyard garden. She looked different than she had six weeks ago. Her hair had lost its sharp precision, her face had more color, and she wasn't wearing the armor of a tailored blazer.

"I need time to think about it," she heard herself say.

"Time to think about a promotion?"

"I'm on leave for a reason, David. My therapist was very clear about the risks of returning to high-stress situations too quickly."

"I understand that. But this is a unique opportunity. If you wait until your sabbatical ends, the Phillips situation will be resolved one way or another. This window closes fast."

Of course it did. Everything in that world closed fast and moved fast. It demanded immediate responses and split-second decisions.

"Give me forty-eight hours," she said.

"Cassidy—"

"Forty-eight hours. That's all I'm asking."

Another pause. "Fine. No longer. But I don't know why you're hesitating. It makes no sense."

She ended the call and set the phone down like it might explode.

Senior VP of Strategy and a corner office. Everything she'd wanted. Everything she'd burned herself out trying to achieve.

She couldn't sit still. The weight of David's offer pressed against her like she'd forgotten how to breathe properly.

She opened her laptop, thinking work might steady her. Not Chicago work. Festival work. The kind that had started to feel less like an obligation and more like a purpose.

The vendor spreadsheet loaded. She scanned the confirmed bookings, the volunteer schedules, and the carefully negotiated contracts that Bryan had helped her navigate. Local fishermen selling their catch. Artists demonstrating traditional net-mending techniques. The Harbor Ladies judging their pie competition with the kind of fierce pride that made corporate award ceremonies look hollow.

This wasn't her world. She'd be gone soon anyway. One week or sooner if she took David's offer.

Her fingers moved to the financial documents almost without conscious thought. Numbers had always been safe. Quantifiable. They didn't ask uncomfortable questions about what she actually wanted from life.

She pulled out her notes again. Attendance

figures from previous decades. Budget allocations. Sponsor lists that showed how the event had evolved from a genuine community celebration to something struggling to justify its own existence.

Then she saw it again. The note she'd made and promptly forgotten in the chaos of final preparations.

Lighthouse funding 1943-1945: Private trust, not government. Check source.

She'd been so focused on the festival that she'd never followed up. Now, with her entire career hanging in the balance and her brain desperately seeking any distraction from that decision, the note pulled at her with professional curiosity.

She opened a new browser tab. Her corporate research skills, honed through years of competitive analysis and market intelligence gathering, kicked in automatically. She started with the basic public records she'd noted before. The lighthouse had officially been privately funded in the 1940s.

The shell company name was buried in a footnote: Coastal Heritage Properties, LLC.

She ran it through the business registry databases she still had access to. The initial search came back with minimal information. Dissolved in 1947. Original incorporation in Massachusetts.

Massachusetts. Not Florida.

That was odd. Why would a Massachusetts

company fund a Gulf Coast lighthouse during wartime?

She dug deeper, following the corporate trail through archived documents and historical business filings. The kind of research that used to make her feel competent and in control when client projects spiraled into chaos.

Coastal Heritage Properties had exactly three listed officers. Two names she didn't recognize. The third made her stop scrolling.

James S. Copeland. Secretary-Treasurer.

Copeland. She'd heard that name recently. Where?

Cassidy pulled up her festival notes, searching through the historical documentation she'd gathered. There. In Marty Fuller's account of the lighthouse's history, mentioned in passing: *The Copeland family of Cambridge maintained a summer residence in Starlight Shores.*

A wealthy Massachusetts family with local connections, funding the lighthouse's private operation. What was their connection?

And that photograph she'd found in the archives. The one that had made Winnie go still and careful. The caption had said academic consultants. Men in suits surrounding radio equipment that had nothing to do with standard lighthouse operations.

Her phone buzzed. A text from Bryan: *One of the*

bands dropped out but the Harbor Ladies found a barbershop quartet to fill in. I think that will work great.

The festival. Right. That's what she should be focused on. Not decades-old mysteries about lighthouse funding and mysterious radio equipment.

Her phone buzzed again. An email from David: *Need to know your decision ASAP.*

Right. Her decision. Her career. Her entire future waiting for a response.

She closed the laptop and walked to the window. Forty-eight hours to choose between everything she'd worked for and everything she was just beginning to discover.

CHAPTER 20

Bryan stood in the kitchen of The Sandpiper, staring at the paperwork for a shipment of produce that should have arrived an hour ago. The delivery truck was late, which meant his morning schedule was already falling apart. He wiped his hands on his apron and checked his phone again.

Nothing from the supplier. Nothing from his loan officer. Nothing from Cassidy.

He told himself that last part didn't matter. She was busy with festival logistics. He was busy running a restaurant, coordinating the fishing schedule, and managing a dozen other things that didn't leave room for checking in with his co-chair every five minutes like some lovesick teenager.

Except he'd been thinking about her every five minutes since they'd danced together at the fundraiser.

"You're hovering again," his mother said from behind him.

"I'm waiting for the produce delivery."

"You're staring at your phone like it personally offended you." His mother moved past him to check the prep station. "That's different."

He shoved the phone in his pocket. "The delivery's late."

"Uh huh." His mother's tone suggested she wasn't buying it, but she let it drop. "Lucy called. She can't cover lunch service today. Her dog is sick. Needs to run him to the vet."

Perfect. Another hole in the schedule. Bryan mentally shuffled staff assignments while his mother continued her inspection of the kitchen. The morning light filtered through the windows overlooking the Gulf, catching on the vintage photographs of fishing boats that lined the walls. His grandfather smiled down from one of those frames, standing on the deck of Mary Catherine with a day's catch spread before him.

What would his grandfather think of the mess Bryan had made of things? The struggling restaurant, the declining catches, and the loan extension still pending. The fact that he'd let himself fall for a woman who'd be leaving soon. Very soon.

"I'll cover lunch," he said.

"You're already working a double."

"I'll manage."

His mother crossed her arms and studied him with the particular intensity that had extracted confessions from him since childhood. "What's going on with you?"

"Nothing's going on. We're short-staffed, and I need to figure out where that produce shipment is."

"I'm not talking about the restaurant."

Bryan turned away to check the walk-in cooler inventory, but his mother followed.

"Bryan Lucas, you look at me when I'm talking to you."

He faced her reluctantly. She'd pulled her graying hair back in a neat bun, and she wore the same determined expression she'd worn when he was sixteen and trying to lie about where he'd been on Friday night.

"I'm fine, Mom."

"You haven't been fine since the fundraiser." She tilted her head. "Or maybe you were fine at the fundraiser. That's the problem. You looked happy for the first time in months, and now you're back to this."

"Back to what?"

"Carrying everything alone." She reached up to pat his cheek. "I saw you dancing with Cassidy. I saw the way you looked at her."

"She's leaving after the festival."

"Is she?"

"Her sabbatical ends. She's got a whole life in Chicago."

"And you've got a whole life here." His mother smiled gently. "Sometimes those things work themselves out. But only if you give them a chance."

The delivery buzzer sounded from the back entrance. Bryan grabbed the opportunity to escape. "That's the produce."

He left his mother shaking her head and went to deal with the late shipment. The driver apologized for the delay, blamed traffic on the coastal highway, and helped Bryan haul the crates in. By the time everything was stored properly and logged into inventory, the morning rush was starting.

Bryan worked the line, falling into the familiar rhythm of prep and plating. The physical work helped quiet his thoughts. He filleted fish, seasoned portions, and coordinated with his line cooks on timing. This he understood. This made sense.

Unlike whatever was happening between him and Cassidy Wren.

The lunch shift blurred past in a haze of orders and coordination. By the time the last table cleared, his feet ached and his shoulders burned from tension. He should go home and sleep before the dinner service. Instead, he found himself walking toward downtown.

Harbor Brew sat on the main road, its large

windows offering a view of the marina beyond. He told himself he was just grabbing coffee, it definitely wasn't that he was hoping to run into Cassidy. It was pure coincidence he was heading to her favorite spot during her usual afternoon work session.

He pushed through the door and scanned the room automatically. The familiar faces of the Harbor Ladies clustered at their usual table. Marty Fuller sat in the back corner with a stack of books. Jan worked behind the counter, chatting with a tourist couple about the best beaches.

And there, at the table in the far corner with her back to the door, sat Cassidy.

Relief flooded through him before he could stop it. She was here. She was still here. Her laptop was open and papers were spread across the table in organized stacks. She held her phone to her ear and nodded at something the person on the other end was saying.

Bryan started toward her table, already imagining her surprised smile when he appeared. Maybe he'd convince her to take a break. They could walk down to the pier, talk about the final festival preparations. Or maybe they'd just sit together and not talk about the festival at all.

He was halfway across the room when her voice carried over the ambient noise.

"Yes, I can have the preliminary framework to you by Monday." She paused, listening. "The target demographic for Phillips skews younger than Marnetti, so we'll want to adjust the messaging strategy accordingly."

He stopped walking.

"Digital integration will be key," she continued. "I'm thinking we lead with social media influencers before the traditional campaign rollout." Another pause. "Yes, sir, the break did me good."

The words hit him hard.

She was going back. Of course, she was going back. Why had he let himself believe anything different?

He turned and walked out before she could see him. The bell above the door chimed his exit, but he didn't look back. His heart hammered against his ribs as he strode down Main Street without any particular destination in mind. His feet carried him toward the marina, toward the one place that had always made sense when the rest of his life fell apart.

The *Mary Catherine* rocked gently at her slip, the afternoon sun warming her deck. He climbed aboard and sat in the captain's chair, staring out at the Gulf without really seeing it.

He'd been such a fool.

All those conversations about her corporate life, the pressure, and burnout. He'd thought she was talking about leaving that behind. He'd thought when she closed her laptop to sit with him on the beach and danced with him at the fundraiser that she was choosing something different.

Choosing here. Choosing this town.

Choosing him.

But she'd just been killing time until her real life started up again. The festival was a portfolio piece. The town was a quaint distraction. And he was what? A pleasant interlude before she went back to big city life and her fancy marketing words?

Bryan's phone buzzed. A text from Cassidy.

Committee meeting at four. Storm system headed our way. Mayor wants to discuss contingency plans.

He stared at the message. Professional. Efficient. Exactly what you'd expect from a co-chair keeping her partner informed.

Nothing more.

He typed back a single word. *Fine.*

His finger hovered over the send button. He wanted to type more. Wanted to ask if she'd already started packing. Wanted to demand why she'd let him fall for her when she knew all along she was leaving.

But that wasn't fair. She'd never promised to stay. She'd been clear from the beginning about her sabbatical having an end date. He was the one who'd built castles in the air, imagining she might want to make a life here.

Bryan deleted the message and typed a new one. *I'll be there.*

Professional and efficient. Exactly what a co-chair should send.

He spent the next hour on the boat, ostensibly checking equipment but mostly just sitting. The sky remained optimistically blue with no sign of the storm system Cassidy had mentioned. The Gulf waters rolled with gentle waves.

But a storm was coming. Of course it was.

At ten to four, Bryan forced himself off the boat and headed to the Bayview General Store. He arrived exactly on time, not early enough to have to make small talk, not late enough to draw attention.

Cassidy was already there, standing near the front with papers in hand and that focused expression she wore when she was in professional mode. She'd pulled her hair back and was wearing one of those crisp blouses she'd favored when she first arrived before she'd softened into linen and casual cotton.

She looked up when he entered and smiled. "Hey. I was hoping we could talk before the meeting starts."

"I'm here for the meeting." He moved past her to take a seat in the back row.

Her smile faltered. "Okay. I just thought we could coordinate on the storm response plan."

"I'm sure you've got it handled."

Mayor West called the meeting to order before Cassidy could respond. He watched her stand at the front, her professional mask firmly in place as she walked everyone through the weather forecast. A storm system was intensifying in the Gulf, expected to make landfall tomorrow, a day before the festival. Heavy rain, high winds, and possible flooding in low-lying areas.

"We need to decide if we're postponing," Mayor West said.

"We can't postpone," Dorothy spoke up. "We've already got vendors traveling in. The tourism board is sending representatives."

"We also can't hold a festival in a tropical storm," Marty pointed out.

Cassidy pulled up a detailed weather map on her laptop. "The storm should pass through quickly. If we're lucky, we can still have the festival as planned."

"That's a lot of contingency planning for a maybe," Bryan heard himself say.

Everyone turned to look at him. Cassidy's expression was carefully neutral.

"The forecast is pretty clear," she said evenly. "We're definitely getting the storm. The question is how we adapt."

"Right. Adaptation." Bryan stood. "That's what you're good at. Adapting to local conditions until it's time to move on to the next project."

Cassidy's eyes widened. "What's that supposed to mean?"

"Nothing. I'm sure you've got the strategy all worked out." He got up and headed for the door. "I've got to get back to the restaurant."

"Bryan, wait." Cassidy started after him, but Mayor West interrupted.

"We really need both co-chairs for this discussion."

Bryan kept walking. He heard Cassidy call his name again, but he didn't stop. He pushed through the door and outside, leaving her to handle the meeting alone.

The way he'd be handling everything alone soon enough.

He made it halfway down the block before his phone started buzzing. Cassidy calling. He declined it and kept walking. She called again. He declined again.

A text appeared: *What was that?*

He shoved his phone in his pocket and headed home. His small house sat three blocks from the waterfront, a modest bungalow that had belonged to his grandmother. He let himself in and stood in the empty living room, surrounded by furniture that had been in his family for generations.

This was his life. This house, the restaurant, the boat, the town. This was what he had to offer.

And it wasn't enough. Not compared to corner offices and big city life.

His phone rang again. This time it was his mother.

"Did you just walk out of the committee meeting?" she demanded.

"I had to get back to the restaurant."

"The one you're not at right now? That restaurant?"

He sank onto the couch. "Mom, I don't want to talk about this."

"But Bryan—"

"I'm fine. Mom, I've got to go." He hung up the phone and turned it off for good measure.

The house felt too quiet. He'd let himself hope. That was the real mistake. He'd let himself imagine that someone like Cassidy Wren might want to build a life in a town like Starlight Shores with a man like him.

But she'd been right that first day they met. He was just a guy trying to hold onto the past while the world moved forward without him.

And she was always meant for bigger things than this small town could offer.

CHAPTER 21

The meeting dissolved into scattered conversations about generator rentals and emergency contact lists. Cassidy watched Bryan's empty chair and felt everyone's careful glances.

Sally appeared at her elbow. "Walk with me."

They stepped outside into air thick with humidity and the promise of the coming storm.

"What was that about?" Cassidy asked.

Sally's face showed the careful neutrality of someone choosing her words. "Dorothy mentioned Bryan stopped by Harbor Brew earlier. Saw you on a phone call." She paused. "He turned around and walked right back out."

Her stomach dropped. The call with David. She'd sat at a corner table for privacy, but she hadn't been hiding. Had Bryan heard her discussing deliverables and implementation timelines? Had he drawn conclusions before she'd even sorted through the mess herself?

"Where does he live?"

Sally gave her the address without hesitation. "Be gentle with him. That boy's been carrying the weight of the world since his daddy died."

She drove through streets she'd learned to navigate without GPS. The cottage Bryan owned sat in a neighborhood of small bungalows with wide porches and mature palm trees. His truck occupied the driveway. Lights glowed inside.

She parked and sat with her hands on the wheel. The smart thing would be to let this go. Give him space. Let the storm pass, literally and figuratively, then approach him when emotions weren't running high.

But she'd spent her entire adult life making the smart choice, the strategic choice, the choice that protected her career at the expense of everything else. Look where that had gotten her.

She climbed out of her car.

The porch light flickered on as she approached. Bryan opened the door before she could knock, standing in the threshold with his arms crossed and his expression carefully blank.

"Mom tell you where I live?"

"Sally, actually." Cassidy held her ground. "We need to talk."

"I think you said everything that needs saying at the meeting."

"I didn't say anything at the meeting. You did."

A muscle worked in his jaw. "You want to come in and discuss storm protocols? Review vendor contracts one more time before you head back to Chicago?"

The bitterness in his voice cut deep.

"I want to understand why you're treating me like I did something wrong."

"You didn't do anything wrong." He stepped back from the door but didn't invite her in. "You were always clear about why you were here. A sabbatical. A temporary arrangement. I'm the fool who forgot that."

She moved forward before he could shut the door. The cottage interior was sparse but comfortable. A worn sofa faced a bookshelf crammed with maritime histories and fishing guides. Framed photographs covered one wall. The Lucas family through the decades, Bryan's father standing proud in front of The Sandpiper's original sign.

"Dorothy said you heard me on the phone this morning."

"Wasn't trying to eavesdrop." He moved to the kitchen and opened the refrigerator, staring at its contents without taking anything out. "Came in for coffee. Heard you talking about digital integration and return dates. Figured it out pretty quick."

"Figured what out?"

He shut the refrigerator and turned to face her. "That this whole thing was exactly what it looked like from the start. High-powered executive takes on small-town project to pad her resume and prove she's still sharp. Returns to her real life with a nice story about how she helped the locals."

"That's not fair."

"Isn't it?" He leaned against the counter. "You showed up here with your color-coded schedules and your marketing expertise, and I was foolish enough to think maybe you actually cared about the festival. About the town." His voice dropped. "About me."

"I do care."

"But not enough to stay."

The truth of it sat between them. "I got a job offer. Senior VP of Strategy. It's everything I've worked toward."

"Congratulations." The word was flat.

"I haven't accepted it."

"But you're going to."

"I don't know."

Bryan's laugh was sharp and humorless. "You don't know. That's great, Cassidy. Real comforting."

She moved closer. "David—my boss—called. One of my colleagues destroyed an account I built from the ground up. They're offering me the corner office, the title, everything I burned myself out trying to earn. They gave me forty-eight hours to give them an answer."

"So you're weighing your options. Seeing if this little coastal town can compete with the big city career." His eyes were hard. "Let me save you some time. It can't."

"That's not what I'm doing."

"He pushed away from the counter. "No? Then what are you doing? Because from where I'm standing, it looks like you're trying to figure out if I'm worth giving up your dreams for. And we both know how that calculation ends."

"You don't know anything about my dreams."

"I know you didn't come to Starlight Shores looking for a life. You came looking for a break. Two months to recharge before you went back to what matters." He gestured around the small cottage. "This was never supposed to be permanent. I get it. I do. But don't stand here and pretend you haven't been planning your exit strategy since day one."

Her hands clenched into fists. "Is that really what you think of me?"

"I think you're terrified of ending up like your mother. Small life, small town, nothing to show for it but regrets." His voice gentled slightly. "And I think you've spent so long running from that fear that you can't recognize when you've found something worth staying for."

The words were too close to the truth. "You don't get to psychoanalyze me."

"Then tell me I'm wrong." He closed the distance between them. "Tell me you haven't been treating the last month like a project with a deadline. Tell me every time we connected, every conversation we had, you weren't already thinking about how it would end."

She wanted to deny it. Wanted to say he was completely off base. But standing in his small kitchen with his hurt written plainly across his face, she couldn't lie.

"I don't know how to do this," she whispered.

"Do what?"

"Let myself want something that doesn't fit into my… plans." Her voice cracked. "I came here broken. The festival was supposed to prove I could still function and still be the person I built my entire identity around being."

"And?"

"Instead, I started caring about things that have nothing to do with deliverables and deadlines." She looked at him. "I started caring about you."

His expression shifted. For a moment, she thought he might reach for her. Then he stepped back and shook his head.

"But not enough."

"That's not fair."

"Fair?" His voice rose. "You want to talk about

fair? I opened up to you. Told you things I haven't told anyone. Let myself believe that maybe, just maybe, you were different. That you saw something in this town, in this life, worth building toward." He ran his hand through his hair. "But no. You look at Starlight Shores like it's a layover between real destinations."

"That's not true." Her anger flared. "I have a career I've sacrificed everything for. My boss is offering me everything I've ever wanted."

"Is he?" He moved toward the door. "Do you want the corner office, or do you want a life, Cassidy? You can't have both."

"Why not?"

"Because the corner office is in Chicago. And the life is here." He opened the door. "And we both know which one you're going to choose."

She stared at him. "I haven't chosen anything yet."

"Yeah, you have. You just don't want to admit it." His face was resigned now, the anger burning out to leave only sadness. "I was falling for you. Really falling. And I thought maybe you felt the same way. But this whole time, I was just the nice distraction before you went back to your real life."

"Bryan—"

"I need you to go."

The dismissal was quiet but absolute. She wanted to argue and tell him he was wrong, that she hadn't been using him, and her feelings were real even if her future was uncertain.

But standing in his doorway with the storm gathering and his hurt filling the space between them, she couldn't find the words.

"I'm sorry," she whispered.

"Yeah." He wouldn't look at her. "Me too."

She walked to her car. Bryan's door closed before she reached the street. She sat behind the wheel and stared at his closed door.

Her phone buzzed. A text from David: *Any thoughts on timing for your return? Team is eager to have you back.*

In the distance, she could just make out the lighthouse beam, steady and constant despite the approaching storm.

Bryan's question echoed in her mind. *Do you want the corner office, or do you want a life?*

The terrible truth was she honestly didn't know.

She'd spent so many years building toward that office. Sacrificed relationships, health, peace of mind. The promotion was validation that all those sacrifices meant something. That she wasn't her mother, settling for less, giving up on ambitions for the comfort of a simple existence.

But the last month or so in Starlight Shores had shown her a different version of herself. Someone who laughed at community fundraisers and learned family recipes. Someone who cared about traditions more than market positioning. Someone who fell asleep without checking email and woke up eager to work on something that mattered for reasons that had nothing to do with her resume.

Someone who was falling for a stubborn fisherman who made her want things she'd never let herself imagine.

CHAPTER 22

Cassidy pulled into the lighthouse parking area. She sat for a moment and watched the lighthouse beam cut through the gathering darkness.

Her phone buzzed again. David, probably. Or Steve with another crisis that somehow required her immediate attention despite the fact that she was supposed to be on leave. She ignored it.

She saw Winnie in the courtyard garden on the bench. She crossed the courtyard, and Winnie looked up and smiled. "I know a storm is coming in, but I thought I'd sit out and enjoy the night air for a bit."

Cassidy looked up at the sky where a few stars poked through the clouds.

"I heard Bryan left the meeting early."

"News travels fast."

"Small town. Dorothy called. Said there was tension between you two."

"He overheard me on a work call. Drew some conclusions."

"What kind of conclusions?"

"That I'm leaving. That this was all temporary. That I was just using the festival to prove I still had what it takes before I went back to my real life." She rubbed her temples. "He's not entirely wrong."

"But is he right?"

"I don't know anymore. When I came here, I had a plan."

"And now?"

"Now my boss is offering me that promotion. Everything I've sacrificed for. He wants an answer in forty-eight hours."

Winnie's expression didn't change. "What do you want to tell him?"

"That's the problem. I don't know." The admission felt like failure. She had built her career on decisive action and clear strategic thinking. Uncertainty was weakness. Hesitation was how you lost ground to competitors.

She shook her head. "I keep making lists. Pros and cons. The salary alone would change my financial trajectory, and if I turn it down, someone else gets that opportunity. There's no guarantee they'd offer it to me again."

Winnie nodded. "Logic is useful. But it's not the whole picture."

"It's the only picture I know how to look at. My mother gave up her career when she married my father. Gave up her ambitions, her education, everything she'd worked for. She settled into a small life in a small town and convinced herself she was happy."

"And you think staying here would make you like her?"

"Wouldn't it? Walking away from everything I've built for a man I've known for a month? For a town that was never supposed to be more than a temporary stop? That's exactly the kind of choice my mom made. The kind she spent the rest of her life regretting."

Winnie was quiet for a moment. "Did you ever ask your mom what she regretted?"

"I didn't have to ask. It was obvious"

"Was it? Or did you decide what her regrets were and build your whole life around avoiding them?"

The question was tougher than she expected. "She gave up everything."

"Maybe. Or maybe she chose something different than what you would have chosen. I'm not saying your mother made the right choice. I don't know her story well enough to say. But I do know that running from someone else's regrets isn't the same as building toward your own happiness."

"I'm not running."

"No? Because from where I'm standing, it looks like you're running from something you weren't expecting to care about."

"The festival will end. Then what? I can't build a career on one successful community event."

"Why not?"

"Because..." She stopped, weary of the same thoughts ping-ponging through her mind.

She deliberately changed the subject. "Oh, I almost forgot. I found something interesting when I was researching the festival finances." She pulled out her phone and opened her notes. "The lighthouse was privately funded during the 1940s through a holding company. I traced the corporate registration. One of the officers was named James S. Copeland."

Winnie's face went carefully blank in a way that reminded Cassidy of high-stakes negotiations where everyone was hiding their cards. "Copeland is a common name," Winnie said.

"From Cambridge, Massachusetts. The same Copeland family that had a vacation home here in Starlight Shores." Cassidy watched Winnie's face. "That seems like an odd connection. A wealthy Massachusetts family funding a Gulf Coast lighthouse during wartime."

"A lot of people have vacation homes here." Winnie's voice was pleasant but distant.

"Right." She got the distinct impression she was being redirected. "I just thought it was interesting."

"I'm sure it's in the historical records somewhere." Winnie picked at an imaginary speck on her skirt.

"Well, I guess I should go in. Hope the storm doesn't get too bad and mess with the festival plans."

"Storms don't always listen to reason." Winnie stood. "Time for me to go in too."

Cassidy headed to Heron Cottage. She stepped inside and flipped on the light. Her phone buzzed again. More messages piling up. David with logistics. Steve Hodges with a passive-aggressive note about transition planning.

The life she'd built was calling her home.

She crossed over to the window and watched the lighthouse beam sweep past. All she could think of was Bryan's face when he'd asked her to leave. She realized something fundamental had shifted. The corner office didn't feel like such a victory anymore.

And she had forty-eight hours—well, less than that now—to decide if she was brave enough to walk away from it.

CHAPTER 23

The first furious wind gusts hit the window of Heron Cottage at six forty-seven in the morning. Cassidy looked up from her laptop, where she'd been staring at the same email for twenty minutes without actually reading it.

The suitcase sat on the floor beside her bed. One blazer lay folded inside, perfectly aligned. She'd managed to pack exactly one item in the two hours she'd been up.

Another gust rattled the windows. The sky had turned an ugly gray-green. She pulled up the weather radar on her phone and watched the angry red blob crawl toward Starlight Shores.

The festival banners were already hung downtown. Three tents had gone up yesterday on the festival grounds. The stage framework stood half-assembled near the harbor.

She closed her laptop and walked to the window. Rain streaked the glass now, coming down harder. She could barely see the lighthouse through the sheets of water.

Her phone buzzed. A text from David Wilde lit up the screen. *Just need confirmation you'll be here Monday for the Phillips meeting. Steve's handling prep, but we need you to close.*

She didn't respond. Instead, she scrolled up to Bryan's last message from yesterday morning. A photo of the sunrise from his boat with the caption: *You missed a great sunrise. Next time you should come with me.*

He hadn't texted since.

The wind howled louder. Something metal clanged in the distance.

She grabbed her jacket from the hook by the door and shoved her feet into the closest shoes she could find. She looked down at her canvas sneakers, which were completely impractical for a storm. She didn't care.

The courtyard was empty when she crossed it, rain soaking through her jacket almost immediately. She could see lights on in Winnie's keeper's quarters, but she didn't stop. She headed to her car and straight into town.

The waterfront was chaos.

People in rain slickers and boots moved in coordinated clusters, securing equipment and hauling supplies. The wind had already torn down one of the banners. It flapped wildly from a single attachment point, cracking like a whip. Two men fought to pull it down before it ripped completely.

She spotted Bryan near the stage, shouting instructions to Cliff and another man she recognized from the harbor. They were wrestling with a tarp that kept trying to fly away.

She ran toward them. The rain pelted her face, and her sneakers squelched in the mud.

"Grab that corner!" Bryan yelled without looking at who had appeared. He pointed to the loose edge of the tarp that was whipping in the wind.

She lunged for it. The wet canvas slipped through her fingers once before she got a solid grip. The wind tried to yank it away. She dug her heels into the soft ground and pulled.

"Tie it off!" Cliff shouted from the other side.

She fumbled with the rope attached to the grommet, her fingers clumsy and cold. The knot her father had taught her for camping trips luckily came back to her. She yanked it tight just as another gust tried to rip everything loose.

Bryan appeared beside her. Water streamed down his face, and his rain slicker was plastered to his shoulders. He stared at her for a long moment.

"I thought you were leaving for Chicago."

"You thought wrong." She had to raise her voice over the wind. "I couldn't leave now. Not like this."

Something shifted in his expression, though she couldn't quite read it through the rain.

"Mom called. The wind shifted, and the deck at The Sandpiper needs securing," he said. "The umbrellas are still up, and the furniture isn't tied down."

"Show me what to do."

They ran together across the waterfront, dodging debris that the wind had already scattered. More people emerged from buildings and vehicles, everyone converging to protect what they could before the worst of the storm hit.

Emily appeared with Melissa, both in proper rain gear and boots. They looked at Cassidy's soaked jacket and muddy sneakers but didn't comment. Emily just handed her a pair of work gloves.

"Thanks." Cassidy pulled them on. They were too big, but they'd keep her hands from getting completely shredded.

At The Sandpiper, Bryan's mother directed traffic from the covered section of the deck. She looked startled when Cassidy appeared but recovered quickly.

"Umbrellas need to come down first," Mona called out. "Then we stack the chairs and tie them to the support posts."

Cassidy moved to the nearest umbrella and started working the crank mechanism. It was stuck. She threw her weight into it, and the handle finally turned. The umbrella slowly descended.

Bryan appeared on her other side and grabbed the pole. Together they maneuvered it out of the table base and carried it to the storage area.

"You're going to ruin those shoes," he said.

"I know."

"And that jacket isn't waterproof."

"I noticed."

They went back for the next umbrella. This one came down easier, but her arms were already starting to ache.

They fell into a rhythm. Melissa and Emily worked on stacking chairs while Cliff secured them with rope. Mona directed and troubleshot. Bryan and Cassidy handled the umbrellas.

The anger that had been crackling between them seemed to dissolve in the shared urgency. They moved like a team. Bryan anticipated where she'd struggle with weight distribution. She learned to read his hand signals through the rain.

"The banner framework downtown is going to go if someone doesn't reinforce it," Cliff called out. He was checking something on his phone. "Wind's only getting worse."

"I'll go," Bryan said immediately.

"I'm coming with you." Cassidy didn't phrase it as a question.

Bryan looked at her again. That same unreadable expression crossed his face. Then he nodded.

They jogged back toward the festival grounds. The rain was coming sideways now. Cassidy could barely see ten feet ahead. Her sneakers had given up any pretense of traction. She slipped twice, and Bryan caught her arm both times without breaking stride.

The banner framework swayed dangerously. Someone had already started working on it. Sally Morris, of all people, was out there with rope, a determined look on her face.

"I've got the north corner," Sally shouted when she saw them. "But the south side is coming loose."

Cassidy ran to the south post while Bryan assessed the damage. The bolts had worked partially free from the ground. The whole structure was listing.

"We need to stake it out more securely," Bryan said. "Cassidy, can you hold this steady while I get the ropes?"

She wrapped both arms around the metal pole. The wind tried to tear it from her grip. Her feet slid in the mud as she braced herself against the force.

Bryan returned with rope and stakes. He worked fast, driving stakes into the ground at angles and running lines from the framework to create tension that would hold it steady.

"On three, let go and step back," he told her.

She counted with him and released. The framework swayed but held. Bryan adjusted the tension on two of the lines, and it steadied.

Sally appeared beside them. She was soaked through but grinning. "Not bad for a city girl."

Cassidy found herself grinning back. "Not bad for a small-town shopkeeper."

"Oh, I like her," Sally told Bryan. "You better not let this one get away."

Bryan didn't respond. He was already moving to check the next vulnerable point.

They worked for another hour as the storm intensified. More volunteers appeared and disappeared. Someone brought thermoses of coffee that tasted like heaven despite being lukewarm. Cassidy lost track of how many things they secured, how many times she slipped in the mud, how many knots she tied with numb fingers.

At some point, Bryan ended up working right beside her again. They were wrestling with a section of fencing that had started to come loose.

"You really aren't leaving?" he asked. His voice was quiet enough that she almost didn't hear it over the wind.

"I don't know." The honest answer came out

before she could stop it. "I don't know what I'm doing."

He didn't say anything for a long moment. They got the fence section secured and stepped back.

"The job offer is real," she continued. She had to tell him. Had to be honest about all of it. "Everything I worked for. Everything I burned myself out trying to achieve."

"I know."

"But I don't know if I want it anymore." The words felt dangerous to say out loud. "I don't know if I ever really wanted it, or if I just wanted to prove I could have it."

He turned to look at her fully. Water dripped from his hair, and his expression was still guarded. Still careful.

"What do you want?" he asked.

The same question he'd asked her before. She still didn't have a complete answer.

"I want to not feel like I'm disappearing when I stop moving," she said. "I want to be part of something that matters. I want to wake up and not immediately check my email to remember who I am."

The wind howled. Thunder rumbled in the distance.

"I want to see how the festival turns out," she added. "I want to know if the tourism board feature actually helps the town. I want to taste whatever your mother is planning to make for the recipe competition."

"Cassidy."

She finally stopped and looked at him.

"I heard you on that phone call," Bryan said. "Talking about digital something or other and returning to work. You sounded like you belonged in that world."

"I know what I sounded like." She pushed wet hair out of her face. "That's the version of me I built. The one who has all the answers and never doubts anything. But I don't think that's who I actually am."

"Then who are you?"

"I'm still figuring that out." She held his gaze. "But I know I'm not ready to leave Starlight Shores yet. I know I'm not ready to walk away from the festival or the people here or—"

She stopped herself. Too much. Too honest.

Bryan's expression shifted. Some of the wariness faded, though not all of it.

"Your sabbatical ends in days," he said.

"I know."

"And then what?"

"I don't know." The frustration in her voice surprised her. "I don't have a plan, Bryan. I don't have a spreadsheet, a strategy, or a five-year forecast. I just know I'm here right now, and I'm not leaving before the festival."

"And after that?"

"I don't know," she repeated. "Can that be enough for now?"

He studied her face. She could see him weighing her words, testing them for truth. Still protecting himself from the possibility that she was just passing through.

"Yeah," he said finally. "That can be enough for now."

The tension between them eased slightly. Not gone, but different. Less sharp.

"Come on," Bryan said. "We should check on the tents one more time, then get you inside and dried off." Then he grinned. "And the next time you go shopping, you should get yourself some proper rain gear."

They walked back toward the festival grounds together. Her sneakers were destroyed, and her jacket was useless. Her hands ached even inside the too-large gloves. And yet, she felt strangely alive. She wasn't watching this town and its people from the outside. She was part of it.

CHAPTER 24

The morning after the storm arrived softly, filtered through the clean-washed air and the quiet murmur of a town assessing its wounds. Cassidy woke to silence instead of wind and stillness instead of chaos. Her body ached in places she didn't know could ache.

She should have felt terrible. Instead, she felt wonderful, alive.

The clock on her nightstand read 6:23 AM. Her phone sat beside it, screen dark and mercifully silent. No urgent pings from David. No passive-aggressive check-ins from Steve. Just blessed, temporary quiet.

She pushed herself upright and winced. Her legs protested the movement. She looked down at her hands, noting the raw patches on her palms, the broken nail on her index finger, and the smudge of what might have been grease or mud or both across her wrist.

These weren't the hands of a Senior VP of Strategy.

She grabbed her phone and pulled on a pair of shorts and one of the t-shirts she'd purchased. Her reflection in the bathroom mirror stopped her cold. Hair was tangled beyond recognition and a streak of something dark crossed her cheekbone. Her eyes looked tired but clear, focused in a way they hadn't been in months.

You look ridiculous.

The thought arrived in David's voice, crisp and dismissive. She could picture exactly how he would say it, with that slight curl of his lip that suggested disappointment without ever stating it outright.

She splashed water on her face and clipped her hair back. She didn't bother with makeup. There was too much to do.

When she got there, the festival grounds looked like a battlefield.

She picked her way across the muddy field, her sneakers squelching with each step. The main stage stood intact but listing slightly to one side. Vendor tents sagged under puddles of collected rainwater. Banners hung askew, their cheerful proclamations about the Harbor Festival now sodden and limp.

But people were already there, working.

Sally Morris directed a small army of volunteers

hauling sandbags away from the general store's entrance. Marty Fuller was up on a ladder, reattaching a section of bunting that had torn loose. Even the Harbor Ladies had arrived, armed with mops, buckets, and an impressive array of cleaning supplies.

"Cassidy!" Dorothy spotted her first, waving from beside a tilted information booth. "Get over here. This thing won't budge."

She jogged over and grabbed one side of the booth. Together with Dorothy and another woman whose name she couldn't remember, she heaved it back into position. The wood was swollen from rain, and it took three tries before the structure finally settled with a wet thud.

"That'll do," Dorothy declared, wiping her hands on her jeans. "Now we just need to dry out everything inside."

"I can help with that," she offered.

Dorothy gave her an appraising look, taking in Cassidy's rumpled clothes and bare face. "You stayed."

It wasn't quite a question.

"I stayed," Cassidy confirmed.

"Good." Dorothy handed her a stack of soggy programs. "Start spreading these out on the picnic tables. Sun's coming out. They might be salvageable."

Cassidy worked steadily for the next hour, falling

into the rhythm of the cleanup. She squeegeed water from table surfaces, carted chairs to the edge of the grounds in hopes the mud would dry up and they could place them around the tables. She helped Cliff set up a new tent. The work was mindless in the best way, requiring just enough focus to keep her hands busy but leaving her thoughts free to wander.

She should call David. She knew that. He'd given her forty-eight hours, and that deadline was approaching fast. The corner office waited, but every time she thought about picking up her phone, something stopped her.

Maybe it was the way Sally had smiled at her when she'd arrived this morning, that warm look of approval that said *you're one of us now*. Maybe it was the ache in her shoulders that came from honest work instead of hunching over a laptop for sixteen hours straight. Maybe it was the memory of Bryan's hand in hers last night, solid and certain even as the storm raged around them.

Or maybe it was simpler than that. Maybe she just didn't want to leave.

"Cassidy!"

She turned to find Bryan jogging toward her, and her heart did a silly, fluttering thing that had nothing to do with exertion. He looked as tired as she felt, his hair sticking up at odd angles and a fresh scrape across his forearm. He was beautiful.

"Hey," she said, aware that she was smiling like

a fool and completely unable to stop. "How's The Sandpiper?"

"Dry. Mostly." He stopped in front of her, close enough that she could smell sawdust and coffee. "Thanks to you."

"I didn't do that much."

"You did everything." His voice was quiet, serious in a way that made her heart skip. "Cassidy, about last night—"

"Mr. Wilde's here to see you."

Cassidy turned to find Jan from Harbor Brew approaching, her expression carefully neutral. "He's waiting by the parking area. Says it's urgent."

The bottom dropped out of Cassidy's stomach.

Bryan's face shuttered closed. "Your boss?"

"I didn't know he was coming," she said quickly. The words tumbled out too fast, too defensive. "I didn't ask him to—"

"It's fine." Bryan took a step back, creating distance that felt like miles. "You should go talk to him."

"Bryan—"

But he was already turning away, heading toward a group of volunteers struggling with a collapsed awning. Cassidy watched him go, her hands clenched into fists at her sides.

She turned and walked toward the parking area, each step feeling heavier than the last.

David Wilde stood beside a sleek black rental

car, looking like he'd stepped out of a boardroom and directly into the wrong century. Pressed charcoal suit. Expensive leather shoes. Phone pressed to his ear as he gestured impatiently at whoever was on the other end of the call.

He spotted Cassidy and ended the call abruptly.

"Finally." He looked her up and down, and his expression flickered through surprise, disdain, and settled on disgust. "Cassidy. You look ridiculous."

The words landed exactly as she'd known they would, sharp and cutting, and designed to make her feel small.

A month ago, they would have worked. A month ago, she would have immediately looked down at herself, cataloging all the ways she'd failed to maintain the polished exterior that David valued.

Now, she just felt tired.

"What are you doing here, David?"

"What do you think? I couldn't wait for an answer." He gestured toward the festival grounds, his lip curling. "I needed to see what could possibly be more important than your career."

She followed his gaze. The muddy field. The sagging tents. The volunteers in their work clothes, hauling debris and wringing out decorations. She tried to see it through his eyes with all the chaos, disorder, and the complete lack of corporate polish.

She couldn't do it. All she saw was community.

Purpose. People who showed up for each other when it mattered.

"This is important," she said quietly.

"This?" David laughed, the sound sharp and dismissive. "Cassidy, this is a small-town fair in the middle of nowhere. The account I'm offering you is worth millions of dollars. Do you understand what that means? Do you have any idea what you're throwing away?"

"I'm not throwing anything away."

"Then prove it. Get cleaned up, and let's go. I'll book the tickets."

He said it like it was already decided and her compliance was a foregone conclusion. Like the past month had been nothing more than an extended vacation, and now it was time for her to come back to reality.

She looked at him—really looked at him—and saw herself reflected back. The version of herself she'd been before Starlight Shores. Always moving, always producing, always terrified that slowing down meant disappearing. She'd thought David was successful. She'd wanted to be him, to earn his respect and prove she belonged in his world.

When had she stopped wanting that?

"I need more time," she said.

David's expression hardened. "I flew down here personally, Cassidy. Do you know what that cost the company? What it cost me?"

"I didn't ask you to come."

"You didn't need to ask. I'm trying to save your career." He stepped closer, and she fought the urge to step back. "You had a meltdown, Cassidy. A public, embarrassing meltdown that could have ended everything. I fought for you. I convinced the board to give you this sabbatical instead of letting you go. And this is how you repay me? By playing festival coordinator in some backwater town?"

The words should have stung. They were designed to sting, to remind her of her lowest moment and make her grateful for his intervention.

Instead, they just made her angry.

"I didn't have a meltdown because I was weak," she said, her voice steady. "I had a problem because I was working myself to death for a company that didn't care if I burned out. For a boss who measures people by their productivity instead of their humanity."

David's jaw tightened. "That's the real world, Cassidy. That's how business works."

"Then maybe I don't want to work in your version of business anymore."

"Don't be naive." He glanced past her, and his expression shifted into something colder. "Is this about him?"

Cassidy turned to see Bryan approaching, his face carefully blank. He carried two bottles of water, and he handed one to Cassidy without looking at David.

"Everything okay?" Bryan asked.

David answered before Cassidy could. "We're having a private conversation."

"Cassidy?" Bryan's eyes stayed on her face, ignoring David completely.

"It's fine," Cassidy said. She took the water bottle, grateful for something to do with her hands. "Bryan, this is David Wilde, my boss. David, this is Bryan Lucas. He's the co-chair of the festival committee."

"The festival committee." David's tone made it sound like she'd said the local garbage collection service. "How impressive."

Bryan's expression didn't change, but recognition flickered in his eyes. He'd met men like David before who looked at people like Bryan and saw nothing worth their time.

"We should probably get back to work," Bryan said to Cassidy. "The stage needs to be secured, and there are more tents to put up."

"Tents!" David shook his head. "Cassidy, get in the car. This is absurd."

"I'm not getting in the car."

"Excuse me?"

"I said I need more time, and I meant it." She straightened her shoulders. "I'll give you my answer when I'm ready. Not before."

"I need you on the Phillips account," he said coldly. "But if not, I'll find someone else."

He didn't wait for a response. He just turned and walked back to his rental car, stepping carefully around a puddle like the water might contaminate his fancy shoes. The engine started with a purr that sounded obscenely out of place against the backdrop of volunteers and cleanup efforts.

She watched him drive away, and her shoulders loosened.

"That's your boss?" Bryan asked after a long moment.

"Unfortunately."

"He seems like a real piece of work."

"He is." She took a long drink of water. "He's also offering me everything I've worked for. A salary I can barely comprehend."

"Then I guess you have a choice to make, don't you?"

The day of the festival, the sun broke through the clouds as if it were singing the Hallelujah Chorus.

Bryan stood at the edge of the harbor, watching the water settle into calm after the storm's fury, leaving behind clear skies and the sharp, clean scent of salt air. Festival banners that had survived the wind snapped cheerfully in the breeze. Volunteers moved through the downtown area, sweeping up any remaining debris and setting up vendor tables with the kind of easy cooperation that came from generations of weathering Gulf storms together.

They'd done it. Despite everything, the Starlight Harbor Festival would open on time.

Pride and relief surged through him, along with a connection that had roots in his grandfather's stories and his father's steady hands teaching him to tie proper knots on the *Mary Catherine's* deck.

"Coffee's ready at the booth if you want some." His mother appeared at his elbow, already dressed in her festival volunteer shirt. She looked tired but satisfied, the way she always did after a long night at The Sandpiper during tourist season.

"Thanks, Mom. I'll grab some in a minute."

"You should eat something too. It's going to be a long day."

"I will."

His mother didn't move. Bryan knew that stance, the particular quality of her silence when she had something to say and was waiting for the right moment to say it.

"What?" he asked.

"Nothing. Just watching my son pretend he's not scanning the crowd for a certain marketing executive."

Heat crept up his neck. "I'm checking the setup. Making sure everything's in place."

"Uh huh." His mother's smile was gentle. "She's over by the main stage. Been there since dawn, organizing the sound check."

Bryan didn't ask how his mother knew who he was looking for. His mother had always possessed an uncanny ability to read her children, a talent that had been both comforting and deeply inconvenient throughout his life.

"I need to check the vendor permits," he said.

"Bryan."

Something in her tone made him stop. His mother reached up and straightened his collar, a gesture so familiar it made his throat ache.

"You know you should tell her," she said quietly.

"Tell her what?"

"How you feel about her."

The words hung in the salt air between them. He looked away, toward the festival grounds where early arrivals were already claiming spots along the parade route. A group of kids chased each other around the gazebo while their parents set up folding chairs. Captain Roy sat on his usual bench, surveying the harbor with the satisfied expression of someone who'd seen seventy festivals and expected to see seventy more.

"It doesn't matter how I feel," Bryan said. "She's got a life in Chicago. A career. That guy showed up yesterday and offered her everything she's worked for."

"And she didn't leave with him."

"Not yet."

"Bryan Lucas, I didn't raise you to be a coward."

The sharpness in her voice made him turn. His mother's eyes were fierce, the same look she'd worn when she'd told him at fifteen that he was going to apologize to the Harrison boy for that ridiculous fight, and again at twenty-three when she'd insisted he was capable of running The Sandpiper after his father's stroke.

"I'm not being a coward," he said. "I'm being realistic. She's got a corner office waiting for her. Everything she's worked years to achieve. What am I supposed to do, ask her to give that up for a struggling restaurant and a fishing boat that barely makes expenses?"

"You're supposed to tell her the truth and let her make her own choice."

"I already know what choice she'll make."

"Do you?" His mother crossed her arms. "Because from where I'm standing, I see a woman who turned down a job offer to stay and finish a festival. Who worked through a tropical storm to help a town she barely knew two months ago. Who looks at you like you hung the moon when she thinks no one's watching."

Bryan's heart kicked against his ribs. "Mom."

"What?"

"Don't."

"Don't what? Don't point out that you're in love with her? Don't mention that she might feel the same way? Don't suggest that you're about to make the biggest mistake of your life by letting her leave without a fight?"

The word hung between them. Love. Bryan hadn't let himself think it, much less say it out loud.

But standing here in the morning sun with the festival coming to life around them, he couldn't deny it anymore.

He loved Cassidy Wren.

Loved her sharp mind and sharper tongue, and the way she'd transformed from a rigid executive in business suits to someone who'd kicked off her heels to wrestle tent poles in a storm. Loved how she listened to Dorothy's recipe stories with genuine interest and how she'd learned every vendor's name. Loved the vulnerability in her eyes when she admitted she didn't know what she wanted, and the fierce determination while she figured it out.

He loved her, and she was probably leaving in two days.

"Even if you're right," he said quietly, "even if she does feel something, I can't ask her to stay. Her whole life is in Chicago."

"Her whole old life? Seems to me she's been building a new one here."

"For two months on a sabbatical. That's not the same as actually choosing this place."

"Then give her a reason to choose it."

He shook his head. "What if I tell her and she leaves anyway?"

"Then at least you'll know you tried." His mother's voice softened. "Baby, I watched you build walls around your heart so nothing sidelines you from what you think is your responsibility to your family. To the town. But maybe it's time to let your guard down. To open up."

Before Bryan could respond, a commotion near the main stage caught his attention. He turned to see David Wilde, Cassidy's boss, standing near the sound booth in the same expensive suit he'd worn yesterday, now slightly rumpled. The man looked profoundly out of place among the festival volunteers in their casual clothes and sun hats.

And there was Cassidy, clipboard in hand, dealing with him.

He couldn't hear the conversation from this distance, but he could read her body language. The straight spine, the professional smile, and the subtle way she angled herself to keep Wilde at arm's length. This was Corporate Cassidy, the version of her he'd met at that first disastrous committee meeting.

Then Sally Morris approached with a question about the recipe competition setup, and everything about Cassidy changed. Her shoulders relaxed, her smile turned genuine, and she touched Sally's arm with easy affection while they talked. When Sally laughed at something Cassidy said, Bryan saw the woman who'd sat at his family's dinner table and charmed his mother with questions about their grandmother's sauce recipe.

Two versions of the same person. The executive and the friend. The corporate strategist and the woman who'd honestly admitted to not knowing what she wanted.

Which one would win?

"You see it too, don't you?" his mother murmured.

He nodded. He saw it. Saw Cassidy navigating between two worlds, two versions of herself. Saw the strain of it in the tight set of her jaw when Wilde said something that made her hands clench on her clipboard.

"I have to get back to the restaurant," his mom said. "Lucy's handling the first shift, but we'll be slammed by noon. But Bryan, listen to me. That woman over there is fighting a battle with herself, and she's doing it alone. Maybe what she needs is someone in her corner. Someone who sees her, really sees her, and wants her anyway. All of her, not just the polished executive or the festival coordinator, but the whole complicated person."

She kissed his cheek and headed toward The Sandpiper, leaving Bryan alone with his thoughts and the growing crowd.

CHAPTER 26

Cassidy stood near the registration tent, clipboard forgotten in her hands as she watched David Wilde circle the festival grounds like a shark in designer shoes. He'd been lurking for an hour now, occasionally checking his watch with theatrical sighs that probably cost extra in whatever leadership seminar taught him that move.

She should have been enjoying this. The festival was exceeding every projection she'd mapped out. Attendance was triple last year's numbers, according to Sally's running tally at the gate. The recipe competition had a waiting list. Grant Stone's local artist showcase was drawing actual buyers, not just browsers. Even the weather had cooperated, delivering the kind of postcard-perfect Gulf Coast afternoon that made tourists forget they had responsibilities back home.

But David's presence turned it all sour. Every time she caught his disapproving scan of the crowd, she felt herself shrinking back into the version of herself that used to care what he thought. The version that would have called this whole event quaint. Charming in a limited demographic sort of way.

She hated that version.

"You look like you're about to snap that clipboard in half." Jan appeared at her elbow with a bottle of water. "Drink. You've been running around for hours."

Cassidy accepted the bottle gratefully. "Is it that obvious?"

"That you're stressed? Honey, you're vibrating." Jan glanced toward David, who was now examining a handmade wreath like it might bite him. "That your boss?"

"Yeah."

"He looks exactly like I pictured. Expensive and uncomfortable." Jan patted her arm. "Don't let him ruin this. Look around. You did this."

She did look around. The harbor glowed in the afternoon light as families wandered between booths, kids clutched cotton candy, and couples shared plates of fried fish from The Sandpiper's booth. The lighthouse rose beyond it all, steady and solid, its white paint almost luminous against the blue sky.

She had done this. With Bryan. With the committee. With a whole town that had somehow decided she was worth trusting.

"Cassidy." David materialized beside her before Jan could escape. "A word."

Jan squeezed Cassidy's hand once and disappeared into the crowd.

"I've been observing," David said, not bothering with pleasantries. "This is impressive for a small market event. You've clearly been allocating significant time and energy here."

"It's a community festival. They needed help."

"And you provided it. Admirably." He adjusted his tie, which had wilted slightly in the humidity. "But this proves my point exactly. You're wasted in a place like this. You should be directing that strategic thinking toward accounts that actually move the needle."

Something in his tone made her grit her teeth. The casual dismissal of everything around them and the assumption that bigger automatically meant better. She used to talk exactly like that.

"David, I told you I need more time."

"And I'm telling you we're out of time. The Phillips team wants an answer by Monday. If you're not in that meeting, Steve gets the position. Permanently."

The threat landed exactly as he intended. Steve Hodges. The man who'd been nipping at her heels for five years, who'd probably celebrated when she burned out. The idea of him getting her promotion made her feel physically ill.

Except…

Except when she tried to picture herself back in Chicago, sitting in that conference room, pitching luxury condos to developers who sounded exactly like George Morton, she couldn't make the image stick. It kept sliding away, replaced by the smell of salt air and fried dough, by the sound of Bryan's laugh carrying across the courtyard last night when Cliff told a terrible fishing story, and by the way Winnie's eyes crinkled when she smiled.

"I understand the stakes," she said carefully. "I'm just not sure they're the stakes that matter anymore."

David's expression hardened. "Don't be naive. This is your career we're discussing. Everything you've worked for."

"I know what I've worked for. I also know what it cost."

She'd never said that out loud before. Never admitted that the corner office might not be worth the price of admission.

David opened his mouth to respond, but something over Cassidy's shoulder caught his attention. His eyes narrowed slightly.

Cassidy turned.

And her heart stopped.

Walking through the festival gates, looking slightly lost but determined, was her mother.

Diana Wren wore a floral skirt and a coral blouse Cassidy had never seen before. Her hair was shorter than the last time she'd seen her, cut in soft layers that framed her face. She carried a large purse and wore sensible sandals, and she was scanning the crowd with the same methodical efficiency Cassidy recognized from her own strategic assessments.

Then their eyes met.

Her mom's whole face transformed. The anxiety smoothed away, replaced by a smile so warm and genuine that Cassidy felt something crack open inside her.

"Mom?" The word came out strangled.

Her mom hurried forward, weaving between families and vendor booths with surprising agility. When she reached Cassidy, she pulled her into a fierce hug that smelled like the clean scent of the soap she'd used for as long as Cassidy could remember.

"Hi, sweetheart," her mom said against her hair. "Surprise."

She pulled back, still gripping her mother's arms like she might disappear. "What are you doing here? How did you even know about the festival?"

"Well..." Her mom glanced past Cassidy, and

her expression shifted into something knowing. "I had some help."

She followed her gaze and found Bryan standing near The Sandpiper's booth, hands shoved in his pockets and looking simultaneously guilty and defiant. When he saw her staring, he offered a small wave.

Her brain struggled to process. "Bryan called you?"

"A week ago. He said you'd been working so hard on this festival, and he thought maybe you'd like some family here to see it. He was very sweet and very worried about overstepping."

A week ago. Before their fight. Before everything fell apart and got *kind of* rebuilt in the space of a single storm.

She looked at Bryan again. He'd turned away now, helping his mother arrange plates at their booth, but his shoulders were tense. He'd called her mom and invited her here because he thought Cassidy would want her.

Because he'd been paying attention.

"I should let you two catch up," David said abruptly. His voice had gone cool and professional. "Cassidy, we'll talk later. Before you make any decisions you'll regret."

He walked away without waiting for a response, already pulling out his phone.

Her mom watched him go and shook her head. "Charming."

"That's my boss. He wants me back in Chicago by Monday."

"And what do you want?"

The question was so simple. So direct. It shouldn't have felt like being punched in the stomach.

"I don't know. I thought I did. The promotion I've been chasing for years is finally on the table. But every time I try to picture myself taking it, I just feel tired."

Her mom studied her face for a long moment. Then she linked her arm through Cassidy's. "Then put it aside for now. Show me this festival you've been working on. I want to see everything."

They walked slowly through the grounds while Cassidy pointed out the different vendors they'd found and the recipe competition judging that would happen in an hour. She pointed to the boat parade route marked with cheerful buoys. She showed her mom the historical display Marty had curated featuring old photographs of previous festivals.

Her mom took it all in with genuine interest, stopping to admire a hand-painted sign here and a vintage fishing net display there. She chatted easily with Sally at the general store booth. She complimented the Harbor Ladies on their baked goods and asked Cliff intelligent questions about lighthouse operations when they passed the small museum display.

She fit in seamlessly, like she'd been coming to this festival for years instead of arriving twenty minutes ago.

"This reminds me of the Mayfair Festival back home," her mom said eventually. They'd found a quiet spot near the water, away from the main crowd. "Do you remember? We used to go every year when you were little."

She felt something shift in her memory. "The one in Indiana. With the craft fair and the pie competition."

"You loved it. You'd make me take you to every single booth, even when your feet hurt. You said you wanted to meet everyone and see everything." Her mom smiled at the memory. "You were so open then. So curious about people."

"I don't remember that part."

"You were. You used to collect stories about the vendors. The woman who made quilts from her grandmother's patterns. The man who carved duck decoys exactly like his father taught him. You said everyone had something important to share."

She watched a family walk past, the parents swinging a toddler between them. "When did I stop thinking that?"

"When you decided their stories didn't scale."

Her mom squeezed her arm gently, but there was no judgment. "When you started measuring value in money instead of meaning."

The words should have stung. Instead, they felt like a relief, like someone finally naming the thing she'd been circling for months.

"I don't know how to stop. I've been running so long, I don't know what happens if I stand still."

"You're standing still right now."

"I'm working. The festival is work."

"Cassidy." Her mom turned to face her fully. "I haven't seen you breathe like this in twenty years."

She opened her mouth to argue, then closed it. Because her mom was right. She was breathing. Deeply and fully, and without the constant tightness in her chest that had become so familiar she'd stopped noticing it.

"This place is doing something for you. I can see it in how you move and how you talk. You're not hitting a performance goal right now. You're just being."

"Being isn't enough. It's never been enough."

"Says who? Your boss? The version of yourself you built to impress people who don't actually know you?" Her mom's voice stayed gentle, but her words cut clean. "Sweetheart, I love you. I have always loved you. But I have watched you disappear into a life that's eating you alive, and I have been terrified that one day you'd wake up and realize you'd spent forty years chasing something that was never going to make you happy."

She felt tears in the corners of her eyes. "You chose small-town life. You chose ordinary. I didn't want that."

"I chose meaning over money and connection over corner offices. And yes, I sacrificed career advancement to do it. But I never once regretted it. I love the life I've built back home. I never wanted you to think my choices meant you couldn't have ambition. I wanted you to have both, and build something you're proud of without losing yourself in the process."

"I don't know if I can have both."

"Maybe not in Chicago. But here?" Her mom gestured to the festival around them. "You've built something extraordinary. You've helped people and made genuine connections. And unless I'm reading things very wrong, you've found something with that handsome restaurant owner who keeps pretending he's not watching us."

She glanced toward The Sandpiper booth. Bryan was definitely not watching them, which meant he absolutely was.

"It's complicated," she said.

"It's only complicated if you make it complicated." Her mom pulled her close again. "You're allowed to want this. You're allowed to choose a life that feels good instead of a life that looks impressive. You're allowed to stay."

Stay.

The word hung in the air between them, terrifying and tempting in equal measure.

She looked around the festival one more time. Really looked. She looked at the families, the vendors, and the lighthouse standing guard over it all. At Bryan, who'd called her mom because he thought Cassidy deserved support. She gazed around at the town that had somehow decided she belonged here.

"I'm scared," she whispered.

"I know." Her mom kissed her forehead. "But you're also braver than you think. And whatever you decide, I'm here. I'm always here."

They stood together while the festival continued around them, and for the first time in as long as she could remember, she let herself imagine a future that didn't involve fighting for the next promotion and looked like Sunday morning coffee at Harbor Brew, sunset walks on the beach, and Bryan's steady presence beside her.

A future that felt like home.

Her phone buzzed in her pocket. Probably David, demanding an answer. Probably Steve, gloating about the promotion he thought he'd won.

She didn't check it.

Instead, she took her mother's hand and led her

toward The Sandpiper booth, where Bryan was trying very hard to look busy with a tray of fried shrimp.

"Bryan," Cassidy said when they reached him. "I'd like you to meet my mom properly."

He looked up, and the vulnerability in his expression nearly undid her. "Mrs. Wren. I'm glad you could make it."

"Call me Diane. And thank you for the invitation." Her mother's eyes sparkled with mischief. "Cassidy tells me you make the best grouper sandwich on the Gulf Coast."

"She said that?" Bryan's gaze found Cassidy's.

"She did. Among other things."

She felt her face heat. "Mom."

"What? I'm just making conversation." Her mom accepted a sample plate from Mona, who'd appeared with impeccable timing. "Oh, this is delicious."

The two mothers immediately began discussing recipes, leaving Cassidy and Bryan standing awkwardly beside the booth.

"You called my mom," she said.

"I thought you'd want her here. For the festival." He rubbed the back of his neck. "I probably should have asked first."

"No. It was perfect." She stepped closer, lowering her voice. "Thank you."

"You're welcome." His eyes searched hers. "Are you okay? Your boss looked pretty intense earlier."

"He wants me in Chicago by Monday."

His jaw tightened, but he nodded. "Makes sense. Big opportunity."

"Bryan—"

"Cassidy, honey!" Sally Morris appeared, slightly breathless. "We need you at the judging table. The recipe competition is about to start, and Dorothy and Margaret are arguing about the scoring criteria."

"I'll be right there." She looked at Bryan helplessly. "I should—"

He nodded. "Go. We'll talk later."

Sally was waiting, the festival needed her, and maybe some conversations were better saved for when they could happen properly.

"Later," she agreed.

She followed Sally toward the judging area but glanced back once. Bryan was watching her go, and even from a distance, she could see the question written across his face.

CHAPTER 27

The festival hit its peak as the sun dipped toward the horizon. Cassidy stood near the main stage, watching families gather blankets and lawn chairs along the waterfront for the boat parade. The scent of fried fish and kettle corn drifted through the warm evening air. Children darted between vendor booths while the Harbor Ladies sold out of their last batch of sweet tea.

She should have felt triumphant. Every metric she'd tracked pointed to success. Attendance had tripled from last year. Local vendors reported record sales. The Gulf Coast Tourism Board representatives had been taking photos all afternoon, already promising feature coverage in their magazine, which would be good publicity for the town.

Instead, her stomach twisted with dread.

David Wilde stood twenty feet away, checking his watch for the third time in as many minutes. He'd changed into khakis and a polo shirt, his concession to casual coastal attire that somehow made him look more out of place than the suit had. Every few minutes, he'd catch her eye and tap his wrist.

The message was clear. Time was running out.

She pulled out her phone. Two missed calls from her office. An email from Steve Hodges that she couldn't bring herself to open. Another text from David: *We need to talk. Now.*

"There you are."

Cassidy turned to find her mother approaching, carrying two cups of lemonade. Her mom had spent the afternoon charming everyone she met, somehow already on a first-name basis with the Harbor Ladies, and deeply engaged in a conversation with Marty about maritime history books.

"I brought reinforcements." Her mom handed her a cup. "You look like you need it."

"I'm fine."

"You're standing like you're waiting for a performance review." Her mom's tone was gentle but firm. "Shoulders back, chin up, braced for criticism."

She forced herself to relax her posture. Her mother was right. She'd reverted to her corporate stance without realizing it, armor against the inevitable confrontation.

"My boss wants an answer."

"I imagine he does." Her mom sipped her lemonade and surveyed the festival grounds. "This is really something, sweetheart. You should be proud."

"It was a team effort."

"Don't do that." Her mom's voice sharpened. "Don't diminish what you accomplished here. You took a struggling event and turned it into something that brought this entire community together. You honored their history while giving them a future. That matters."

She wanted to believe that. Wanted to think the past six weeks had been more than just a portfolio piece or a sabbatical project. But David's presence reminded her of the cost of that belief.

The corner office. The title she'd spent years chasing. The validation that she was good enough, successful enough, and that the burnout hadn't broken her permanently.

If she walked away now, it would all be gone.

"Mom, I don't know what to do."

"Yes, you do. You're just afraid to admit it."

Before she could respond, David materialized beside them. His smile was pleasant, but his eyes were cold.

"Mrs. Wren, lovely to see you again." He barely

glanced at her mom before focusing on Cassidy. "I need to borrow Cassidy for a moment. Business."

"Actually, we were just—"

"It won't take long." David's hand closed around Cassidy's elbow, already steering her away.

She met her mother's gaze. Her mom's expression was calm, but her meaning was clear. *This is your choice. Make it.*

David guided her toward the pier, away from the crowds. The festival noise faded behind them, replaced by the gentle lap of water against the pilings and the distant cry of gulls. The sun hung low on the horizon, spilling splashes of amber and violet over the Gulf.

It should have been beautiful. Instead, she felt like she was walking to her execution.

David stopped at the end of the pier and released her arm. When he turned to face her, all pretense of pleasantness had vanished.

"I've been patient, Cassidy. More than patient. But this ends now."

She crossed her arms. "The festival isn't over for another two hours."

"I'm not talking about the festival. I'm talking about this ridiculous sabbatical fantasy." He gestured dismissively at the town behind them. "You've had your break. You've played small-town hero. Now it's time to come back to reality."

"This is reality."

"This?" He laughed, sharp and cutting. "This is a dying fishing village desperately clinging to relevance. You organized a nice little fair for them. Congratulations. But don't confuse a successful event with a sustainable future."

She looked at him defiantly. "The Gulf Coast Tourism Board thinks differently."

"The Tourism Board wants content for their brochures. They'll feature you for one season and move on to the next quaint coastal town." He stepped closer. "But I'm offering you a career. The Senior VP position. Your own division and everything that comes after it. That's real power, Cassidy. Real influence. Not this small-time nonsense."

"This small-time nonsense matters to people."

"People like Bryan Lucas?" David's smile turned cruel. "The fisherman playing at restaurant owner? You think he's going to provide the kind of life you're accustomed to? The kind of challenge that actually uses your talents?"

Heat flooded Cassidy's face. "Bryan has nothing to do with this decision."

"Doesn't he?" David pulled out his phone and swiped through screens. "I did some research while you were busy playing event coordinator. The Sandpiper is hemorrhaging money. Lucas took out a second mortgage last year, and he's behind on payments. His fishing operation is underwater, metaphorically and soon literally, when Oceanside Development buys up the waterfront."

She had known Bryan was struggling, but hearing it laid out so clinically made her stomach churn.

"You're a brilliant strategist, Cassidy. Surely you can see the math here." David's voice softened to something almost sympathetic. "This town is dying. Your fisherman is failing. And you're standing here pretending that a few weeks of playing house changes years of building a career."

"I'm not playing house."

"Then what are you doing?" He spread his hands. "Because from where I'm standing, you're throwing away everything you worked for. Everything you are. For what? A man you barely know and a town that will forget you exist the moment the next crisis hits?"

She wanted to argue, tell him he was wrong, and that he didn't understand what she'd found here. But the words caught in her throat because part of her wondered if he was right.

She'd been in Starlight Shores for eight weeks. Eight weeks against all those years in Chicago. Eight weeks of borrowed community and temporary purpose. What made her think she belonged here? That she could build a real life in a place where she'd arrived as a stranger?

The lighthouse beam swept across the water, its

steady rotation marking time. She watched the light arc through the gathering dusk and thought about Bryan's grandfather's words. *The light shows you where you are, not just where you're going.*

Where was she?

Standing on a pier in a town that had welcomed her when she had nothing to offer but broken ambition and empty schedules. A town that had trusted her with their history and their future. A town that had given her friendship and community and the first real peace she'd felt in years.

A town where Bryan Lucas had looked at her like she mattered for more than her quarterly performance metrics.

"I need an answer, Cassidy." David's patience was fraying. "We can be back in Chicago by midnight if we leave now. You can spend the rest of the weekend preparing for Monday's meeting. Steve will be there, of course, eager to take credit for saving the Phillips account. Unless you're there to remind everyone exactly who built that relationship in the first place."

The familiar competitive fire sparked in her chest. Steve Hodges, with his smug emails and calculated undermining, sitting in her seat at the conference table and taking credit for her work. She'd given the company fifteen years of her life, and they'd responded to her burnout by putting her on mandatory leave and letting her rival circle like a shark.

The Cassidy who'd arrived in Starlight Shores would have been terrified of that and jumped at the chance to reclaim her position and prove she was still sharp, still valuable.

But that Cassidy had been running on empty, measuring her worth in titles and metrics because she had nothing else to measure.

This Cassidy had spent the morning helping Sally Morris hang bunting and laughed with Dorothy and the Harbor Ladies over recipe cards. She'd watched Mona Lucas beam with pride as festival-goers lined up for The Sandpiper's booth. She'd felt her mother's hand squeeze hers as they surveyed the crowded grounds together.

She had fallen in love with a man who saw past her resume to the person she was becoming.

The realization settled over her like the lighthouse beam, steady and undeniable.

She turned to face him fully. "I'm not coming back."

His expression flickered with surprise before hardening. "Excuse me?"

"I appreciate the offer. I really do. But I'm not coming back to Chicago." The words felt strange in her mouth, both terrifying and liberating. "I'm staying in Starlight Shores."

"Cassidy, don't be ridiculous. You can't just—"

"And yet, I can."

David looked startled, and she took the opportunity to move past him, putting distance between them.

"You're making a mistake," he called after her. "You think this town wants you? You're a project to them. A consultant they'll use until the novelty wears off. Then what? You'll come crawling back to Chicago, but the opportunity will be gone. Steve will have your office, your accounts, and your future."

She paused and looked back at him. The man who'd once represented everything she aspired to now looked small and petty against the backdrop of the festival and the life she was choosing.

"Maybe," she said quietly. "But I don't care. I know I'm making the right choice."

She walked away without waiting for his response.

The festival had transformed in her absence. The boat parade was forming up in the harbor, with vessels of every size decorated with strings of lights that glimmered in the deepening twilight. Families clustered along the waterfront, and children perched on parents' shoulders to get a better view. The air hummed with anticipation and joy.

Cassidy found her mother near the quilt display, standing beside Winnie and admiring an intricate wedding ring quilt.

"That was quick," her mom said, studying Cassidy's face. "Everything okay?"

"I quit."

Winnie's eyebrows rose, but she said nothing. Her mom's expression shifted from surprise to pride.

"No job, no plan," she continued, the words spilling out faster now. "I have no idea what I'm going to do for work or where I'm going to live when my rental ends or how any of this is going to work out. But I couldn't get in that car. I couldn't go back to being the person I was in Chicago."

Her mom pulled her into a tight hug. "I'm so proud of you."

"I might have just ruined my entire career."

"Or you just saved your life." Her mom pulled back, keeping her hands on Cassidy's shoulders. "The details will work themselves out. They always do. Right now, I think there's someone you need to talk to."

She nodded toward the dock where Bryan stood alone, checking the moorings one final time before the parade began. He hadn't changed from his work clothes, still wearing the faded shorts and Sandpiper t-shirt he'd had on all day. His hair was disheveled from running his hands through it, a habit she'd learned meant he was worried.

He was strikingly handsome.

"Go," her mom said gently. "Winnie and I have quilts to admire."

Her feet carried her toward the dock before her brain could catalog all the reasons this was terrifying. Bryan looked up as she approached, his expression cautious.

"Hey." His voice was careful and guarded. "Festival's going well."

"It is."

They stood in awkward silence. The easy partnership they'd developed over the past weeks felt fragile now, full of everything unsaid between them.

She took a breath. "I quit my job."

Bryan went very still. "What?"

"David wanted me to leave tonight. Fly back to Chicago." The words tumbled out faster. "I told him no. I'm not ever going back. I'm staying here. I don't know for how long or what I'm going to do, but I'm not leaving. Not yet. Maybe not ever. I know that's crazy and impractical and probably the worst career decision I've ever made, but—"

"Cassidy."

She stopped, breathless.

He took a step closer. Then another. In the fading light, his eyes were impossibly warm. "Cassidy, stop for one minute. Please. I just have to tell you something."

"What?"

"I love you."

"You… What did you say?"

"I'm in love with you. Have been for weeks, probably. I was just too scared to say it because I thought you were going to leave." He reached for her hands. "I know you just quit your job, and everything's uncertain, but I need you to know. I love you. The real you. Not the corporate executive or the festival coordinator. Just you."

Tears gathered in her eyes. "I don't have a plan."

"Neither do I. We'll figure it out together."

"I'm probably going to panic about this decision at least six times before morning."

"I'll be there for all six. You don't have to have everything figured out. You just have to be here."

Behind them, the first boats in the parade began their slow procession through the harbor. Lights reflected off the dark water, creating ribbons of gold and silver.

Bryan drew her closer. "Now, can I finally kiss you?"

In answer, she closed the distance between them.

The kiss was soft at first. Tentative. Then his hand came up to cup her face, and she melted into him, all the fear and uncertainty of the past weeks dissolving into this perfect moment. The festival lights showered them with warm colors. The sound of cheering from the crowd at the parade filtered through her awareness like music.

He finally pulled back slightly. "Ummm, that was... nice."

She grinned up at him. "It was." Then she glanced over and saw her mom and Mona watching them, smiles on their faces. "Looks like our moms approve."

He glanced over and laughed. "Let's give them something more to talk about." He kissed her again.

When they finally broke apart, Bryan rested his forehead against hers.

"Welcome home," he whispered.

She looked past him to the lighthouse, its beam sweeping steadily through the night. Then back to the festival grounds where their moms stood, both women watching with knowing smiles.

Home. The word settled over her, fitting perfectly into a space she hadn't known was empty.

"Yeah," she said softly. "I think I am."

CHAPTER 28

The crowd thinned as the last night of the festival drew to a close. Winnie stood at the edge of the festival grounds, far enough from the stage lights that the shadows gave her room to breathe. The celebration had exceeded every expectation. Laughter still bubbled up from clusters of families gathered around the fire pits, and the scent of fried dough and salt air mingled in the warm evening breeze.

The festival had brought the community together in ways she hadn't seen in years. Cassidy had accomplished something remarkable, breathing new life into a tradition that had been gasping for air, and Bryan looked happier than Winnie had seen him since his father passed.

Sally appeared at her elbow and threaded her arm through Winnie's. "You did good, Win."

"I didn't do anything."

Sally nodded toward Cassidy, who stood near the dock with Bryan, their heads bent close together. "You knew what she needed before she did."

She watched the young couple. Cassidy's laugh carried across the water, genuine and unguarded. Bryan's hand rested on the small of her back like it belonged there. The lighthouse beam swept past them, illuminating their faces for just a moment before moving on.

"They found each other," Winnie said quietly. "I just provided the cottage."

"You always were terrible at taking credit." Sally squeezed her arm. "Remember when you organized the entire Hurricane Relief effort in ninety-eight and told everyone it was a community effort?"

"It was a community effort."

"You coordinated sixteen volunteer groups and raised forty thousand dollars in three weeks."

She smiled despite herself. "Ancient history."

They stood in comfortable silence as the festival volunteers began breaking down booths and hauling equipment toward the storage shed. Mayor West waved from across the courtyard, triumph written across her face. Winnie waved back.

"You think she'll stay?" Sally asked. "Cassidy?"

"Yes, she's already decided to." Winnie studied the way Cassidy leaned into Bryan and the way her shoulders had finally relaxed after weeks of carrying invisible weight. "She just needed to figure out what home felt like."

"That's what you do best. Helping people find home."

The words settled uncomfortably over her. She'd spent so many years creating homes for others while her own remained carefully curated and impeccably empty. The keeper's quarters held generations of Lockhart history, but precious little of her own story. Just photographs, logbooks, and secrets she couldn't share and didn't fully understand.

The crowd shifted as a group of teenagers rushed past, chasing each other toward the beach. In the space they left behind, Winnie saw him.

Her breath caught.

He stood near the harbormaster's office, partially obscured by the corner of the building. Tall. Older now, his dark hair threaded with silver. But she would know those shoulders anywhere, the way he held himself with quiet confidence. Distinguished, her mother would have said. Handsome in a way that had nothing to do with youth and everything to do with character worn gracefully.

Sam Copeland.

The world narrowed to just him. Everything else faded. The music, the laughter, the gentle lap of waves against the dock. Gone. There was only the man who had left Starlight Shores over forty-five years ago and taken a piece of her heart with him.

Sally's grip on her arm tightened. "Win?"

She couldn't answer. Couldn't breathe properly. Her hand drifted to the bracelet at her wrist, fingers finding the familiar shape of the sea glass embedded in the silver wire. He'd made it for her that summer before everything fell apart, and duty demanded she choose the lighthouse over love. Before she'd stood on this same beach and watched him walk away.

Sam's gaze swept the festival crowd like he was searching for something. Someone.

"Is that..." Sally's voice trailed off.

"Yes."

"Sam Copeland. After all this time."

"Yes." The word barely made it past her throat.

He looked good. Older, yes, but good. Strong. Certain.

Everything she wasn't in this moment.

Then he was gone, disappearing into the thinning crowd.

Winnie stood with Sally, one hand pressed to her racing heart, the other still clutching the bracelet he'd made her a lifetime ago.

The past she'd buried had come walking back into town.

And she had no idea what to do about it.

∾

Dear Reader, I hope you enjoyed this addition to the Starlight Shores series. Next up is Coastal Shadows. (This is Melissa and Cliff's book.)

In the *Coastal Shadows*, a photographer hiding from a single life-changing moment takes refuge at the town's lighthouse. But between a gruff handyman, a watchful seaside community, and the steady beam of the lighthouse itself, she may discover that the safest place to hide is also the place she was meant to heal.

As always, thank you for reading my books. I hope you're enjoying the Starlight Shores series. And there's more to come!

Happy reading. ~Kay

COMFORT CROSSING ~ THE SERIES

The Shop on Main - Book One

The Memory Box - Book Two

The Christmas Cottage - A Holiday Novella (Book 2.5)

The Letter - Book Three

The Christmas Scarf - A Holiday Novella (Book 3.5)

The Magnolia Cafe - Book Four

The Unexpected Wedding - Book Five

The Wedding in the Grove (crossover short story between series - Josephine and Paul from The Letter.)

LIGHTHOUSE POINT ~ THE SERIES

Wish Upon a Shell - Book One

Wedding on the Beach - Book Two

Love at the Lighthouse - Book Three

Cottage near the Point - Book Four

Return to the Island - Book Five

Bungalow by the Bay - Book Six

Christmas Comes to Lighthouse Point - Book Seven

CHARMING INN ~ Return to Lighthouse Point

One Simple Wish - Book One

Two of a Kind - Book Two

Three Little Things - Book Three

Four Short Weeks - Book Four

Five Years or So - Book Five

Six Hours Away - Book Six

Charming Christmas - Book Seven

SWEET RIVER ~ THE SERIES

A Dream to Believe in - Book One

A Memory to Cherish - Book Two

A Song to Remember - Book Three

A Time to Forgive - Book Four

A Summer of Secrets - Book Five

A Moment in the Moonlight - Book Six

MOONBEAM BAY ~ THE SERIES

The Parker Women - Book One

The Parker Cafe - Book Two

A Heather Parker Original - Book Three

The Parker Family Secret - Book Four

Grace Parker's Peach Pie - Book Five

The Perks of Being a Parker - Book Six

BLUE HERON COTTAGES ~ THE SERIES

Memories of the Beach - Book One

Walks along the Shore - Book Two

Bookshop near the Coast - Book Three

Restaurant on the Wharf - Book Four

Lilacs by the Sea - Book Five

Flower Shop on Magnolia - Book Six

Christmas by the Bay - Book Seven

Sea Glass from the Past - Book Eight

MAGNOLIA KEY ~ THE SERIES

Saltwater Sunrise - Book One

Encore Echoes - Book Two

Coastal Candlelight - Book Three

Tidal Treasures - Book Four

Bayside Beginnings - Book Five

Seaside Sunshine - Book Six

Boardwalk Breezes - Book Seven

STARLIGHT SHORE ~ THE SERIES

Lighthouse Cottages - Book One

Harbor Festival - Book Two

CHRISTMAS SEASHELLS AND SNOWFLAKES

Seaside Christmas Wishes

Sweet River Holiday Homecoming

WIND CHIME BEACH ~ A stand-alone novel

INDIGO BAY ~

Sweet Days by the Bay - Kay's complete collection of stories in the Indigo Bay series

ABOUT THE AUTHOR

Kay Correll is a USA Today bestselling author of sweet, heartwarming stories that are a cross between women's fiction and contemporary romance. She is known for her charming small towns, quirky townsfolk, and the enduring strong friendships between the women in her books.

Kay splits her time between the southwest coast of Florida and the Midwest of the U.S. and can often be found out and about with her camera, taking a myriad of photographs, often incorporating them into her book covers. When not lost in her writing or photography, she can be found spending time with her ever-supportive husband, knitting, or playing with her puppies—a cavalier who is too cute for his own good and a naughty but adorable Australian shepherd. Their five boys are all grown now and while she misses the rowdy boy-noise chaos, she is thoroughly enjoying her empty nest years.

Learn more about Kay and her books at kaycorrell.com

While you're there, sign up for her newsletter to hear about new releases, sales, and giveaways.

WHERE TO FIND ME:
My shop: shop.kaycorrell.com
My author website: kaycorrell.com
authorcontact@kaycorrell.com

Join my Facebook Reader Group. We have lots of fun and you'll hear about sales and new releases first!
www.facebook.com/groups/KayCorrell/

I love to hear from my readers. Feel free to contact me at authorcontact@kaycorrell.com

facebook.com/KayCorrellAuthor

instagram.com/kaycorrell

pinterest.com/kaycorrellauthor

amazon.com/author/kaycorrell

bookbub.com/authors/kay-correll